EUCALYPTUS

"There is such delight in *Eucalyptus*, such strange and sly and swerving humour. Murray Bail is the warmest and most quick-witted of storytellers. You will never forget what is at the heart of this book: one of the great and most surprising courtships in literature"   MICHAEL ONDAATJE

"It's a masterpiece. A novel of high seriousness and higher playful-ness that will scarcely be matched this year for the dexterity of its wit"   MICHAEL HULSE, *Spectator*

"*Eucalyptus* is that rare thing: a book whose author has succeeded in harnessing the seductive format of the fairy story and trans-forming it into something quite distinctive – neither fantastical nor realistic, but an elegant, humane, funny and wise journey to the interior of the human heart"

JANE SHILLING, *Sunday Telegraph*

"It's a pleasure simply to be immersed in Bail's caprice-prone mind. *Eucalyptus* with its pixilated wit and technical wizardry, is storytelling as deliberate as it comes. But the only warning readers need is that it leaves you hungering for more – far more – of its author's strange and spry imaginings"

MICHAEL UPCHURCH, *New York Times*

"Beautiful in its persistent interconnectedness, Bail's third novel is something like a guide to the marvellous preoccupations of ordinary folk as they pick their way through life with a mixture of ingenuity and originality . . . an astonishing achievement"

ALISON HUNTLY, *Independent*

MURRAY BAIL was born in Adelaide in 1941, and now lives in Sydney. His first novel, *Homesickness*, won the National Book Award for Australian Literature and the *Melbourne Age* Book of the Year Award. His subsequent novel, *Holden's Performance*, won the Vance Palmer Prize for Fiction. His non-fiction includes an acclaimed monograph on the work of the painter Ian Fairweather.

Also by Murray Bail

THE DROVER'S WIFE AND OTHER STORIES

HOMESICKNESS

HOLDEN'S PERFORMANCE

———

THE FABER BOOK OF CONTEMPORARY
AUSTRALIAN SHORT STORIES (EDITOR)

Non-fiction

IAN FAIRWEATHER

LONGHAND: A WRITER'S NOTEBOOK

Murray Bail

EUCALYPTUS

THE HARVILL PRESS
LONDON

First published by The Text Publishing Company, Melbourne in 1998

First published in Great Britain in 1998

This paperback edition first published in 1999 by
The Harvill Press, 2 Aztec Row, Berners Road, London N1 0PW

www.harvill-press.com

1 3 5 7 9 8 6 4 2

Copyright © Murray Bail, 1998

Murray Bail asserts the moral right to be identified as the author of this work

A CIP catalogue record for this book is available from the British Library

ISBN 1 86046 495 5

Printed and bound in Great Britain by Mackays of Chatham

Half title: photograph by Richard Haughton

EUCALYPTUS

1

Obliqua

WE COULD BEGIN with *desertorum*, common name Hooked Mallee. Its leaf tapers into a slender hook, and is normally found in semi-arid parts of the interior.

But *desertorum* (to begin with) is only one of several hundred eucalypts; there is no precise number. And anyway the very word, *desert-or-um*, harks back to a stale version of the national landscape and from there in a more or less straight line on to the national character, all those linings of the soul and the larynx, which have their origins in the *bush*, so it is said, the poetic virtues (can you believe it?) of being belted about by droughts, bushfires, smelly sheep and so on; and let's not forget the isolation, the exhausted shapeless women, the crude language, the always wide horizon, and the flies.

It is these circumstances which have been responsible for all those extremely dry (dun-coloured – can we say that?) hard-luck stories which have been told around fires and on the page. All that was once upon a time, interesting for a while, but largely irrelevant here.

Besides, there is something unattractive, unhealthy even, about *Eucalyptus desertorum*. It's more like a bush than a tree; has hardly a trunk at all: just several stems sprouting at ground level, stunted and *itchy*-looking.

We might as well turn to the rarely sighted *Eucalyptus pulverulenta*, which has an energetic name and curious heart-shaped leaves, and is found only on two narrow ledges of the Blue Mountains. What about *diversifolia* or *transcontinentalis*? At least they imply breadth and richness of purpose. Same too with *E. globulus*, normally employed as a windbreak. A solitary specimen could be seen from Holland's front verandah at two o'clock, a filigree pin of greyish-green stuck stylishly in a woman's felt hat, giving stability to the bleached and swaying vista.

Each and every eucalypt is interesting for its own reasons. Some eucalypts imply a distinctly feminine world (Yellow Jacket, Rose-of-the-West, Weeping Gum). *E. maidenii* has given photogenic shade to the Hollywood stars. Jarrah is the timber everyone professes to love. *Eucalyptus camaldulensis*? We call it River Red Gum. Too masculine, too overbearingly masculine; covered in grandfatherly warts and carbuncles, as well. As for the Ghost Gum (*E. papuana*), there are those who maintain with a lump in their throats it is the most beautiful tree on earth, which would explain why it's been done to death on our nation's calendars, postage stamps and tea-towels. Holland had one marking the north-eastern corner, towards town, waving its white arms in the dark, a surveyor's peg gone mad.

We could go on forever holding up favourites or returning to botanical names which possess almost the right resonance or offer some sort of summary, if such a thing were possible, or which are hopelessly wide of the mark

but catch the eye for their sheer linguistic strangeness –
platypodos; whereas all that's needed, aside from a beginning
itself, is a eucalypt independent of, yet one which . . . it
doesn't really matter.

Once upon a time there was a man – what's wrong with
that? Not the most original way to begin, but certainly tried
and proven over time, which suggests something of value,
some deep impulse beginning to be answered, a range of
possibilities about to be set down.

There was once a man on a property outside a one-horse
town, in New South Wales, who couldn't come to a decision
about his daughter. He then made an unexpected decision.
Incredible! For a while people talked and dreamed about
little else until they realised it was entirely in keeping with
him; they shouldn't have been surprised. To this day it's
still talked about, its effects still felt in the town and
surrounding districts.

His name was Holland. With his one and only daughter
Holland lived on a property bordered along one side by a
khaki river.

It was west of Sydney, over the ranges and into the sun –
about four hours in a Japanese car.

All around, the earth had a geological camel-look: slowly
rearing brown, calloused and blotched with shadows, which
appeared to sway in the heat, and an overwhelming air
of patience.

Some people say they remember the day he arrived.

It was stinking hot, a scorcher. He stepped off the train
alone, not accompanied by a woman, not then. Without
pausing in the town, not even for a glass of water, he went

out to his newly acquired property, a deceased estate, and began going over it on foot.

With each step the landscape unfolded and named itself. The man's voice could be heard singing out-of-tune songs. It all belonged to him.

There were dams the colour of milky tea, corrugated sheds at the trapezoid tilt, yards of split timber, rust. And solitary fat eucalypts lorded it over hot paddocks, trunks glowing like aluminium at dusk.

A thin man and his three sons had been the original settlers. A local dirt road is named after them. In the beginning they slept in their clothes, a kelpie or wheat bags for warmth, no time for the complications of women – hairy men with pinched faces. They never married. They were secretive. In business they liked to keep their real intentions hidden. They lived in order to acquire, to add, to amass. At every opportunity they kept adding, a paddock here and there, in all directions, acres and acres, going into hock to do it, even poxy land around the other side of the hill, sloping and perpetually drenched in shadow and infected with the burr, until the original plot on stony ground had completely disappeared into a long undulating spread, the shape of a wishbone or a broken pelvis.

These four men had gone mad with ring-barking. Steel traps, fire, and all types of poisons and chains were also used. On the curvaceous back paddocks great gums slowly bleached and curled against the curve as trimmings of fingernails. Here and there bare straight trunks lay scattered and angled like a catastrophe of derailed carriages. By then the men had already turned their backs and moved on to the next rectangle to be cleared.

When at last it came to building a proper homestead they built it in pessimistic grey stone, ludicrously called *bluestone*, quarried in a foggy and distinctly dripping part of Victoria. At a later date one of the brothers was seen painting a wandering white line between the brick-courses, up and along, concentrating so hard his tongue protruded. As with their land, bits were always being tacked on – verandahs, outhouses. To commemorate dominance of a kind they added in 1923 a tower where the four of them could sit drinking at dusk and take pot shots at anything that moved – kangaroos, emus, eagles. By the time the father died the property had become one of the district's largest and potentially the finest (all that river frontage); but the three remaining sons began fighting among themselves, and some of the paddocks were sold off.

Late one afternoon – in the 1940s – the last of the bachelor-brothers fell in the river. No one could remember a word he had said during his life. He was known for having the slowest walk in the district. He was the one responsible for the infuriating system of paddock gates and their clumsy phallic-fitting latchbolts. And it was he who built with his bare hands the suspension bridge across the river, partly as a rickety memorial to the faraway world war he had missed against all the odds, but more to allow the merinos with their ridiculous permed parted heads to cross without getting their feet wet when every seven years floodwaters turned the gentle bend below the house into a sodden anabranch. For a while it had been the talk of the district, its motif, until the next generation saw it as an embarrassment. Now it appears in glossy books produced in the distant city to illustrate the ingenious, utilitarian nature of folk art: four cables slung between two trees, floored with cypress, laced with fencing wire.

In the beginning Holland didn't look like a countryman, not to the men. Without looking down at his perforated shoes they could tell at once he was from Sydney. It was not one thing; it was everything.

To those who crossed the street and introduced themselves he offered a soft hand, the proverbial fish itching to slip out under the slightest pressure. He'd smile slightly, then hold it like someone raising a window before committing himself. People didn't trust him. The double smile didn't help. Only when he was seen to lose his temper over something trivial did people begin to trust him. The men walking about either had a loose smile, or faces like grains of wheat. And every other one had a fingertip missing, a rip in the ear, the broken nose, one eye in a flutter from the flick of the fencing wire. As soon as talk moved to the solid ground of old machinery, or pet stories about humourless bank managers or the power of certain weeds, it was noticed that although Holland looked thoughtful he took no part.

Early on some children had surprised him with pegs in his mouth while he was hanging the washing, and the row of pegs dangling like camel teeth gave him a grinning illiterate look. Actually he was shrewd and interested in many things. The word was he didn't know which way a

8

gate opened. His ideas on paddock rotation had them grinning and scratching their necks as well. It made them wonder how he'd ever managed to buy the place. As for the perpetually pissing bull which had every man and his dog steering clear of the square back-paddock he solved that problem by shooting it.

It would take years of random appearances in all weather, at arm's length and across the street, before he and his face settled into place.

He told the butcher's wife, "I expect to live here for seven years. Who knows after that?" Catching the pursing of her Presbyterian lips he added, "It's nice country you've got here."

It was a very small town. As with any new arrival the women discussed him in clusters, turning to each other quite solemnly. Vague suggestions of melancholy showed in the fold of their arms.

They decided there had to be a woman hidden away in a part of his life somewhere. It was the way he spoke, the assumptions settled in his face. And to see him always in his black coat without a hat walking along the street or at the Greek's having breakfast alone, where nobody in their right mind took a pew and ate, was enough to produce in these dreaming women elongated vistas of the dark-stone homestead, its many bare rooms, the absence of flowers, all those broad acres and stock untended – with this man, half-lost in its empty dimensions. He appeared then as a figure demanding all kinds of attention, correction even.

A certain widow with florid hands made a move. It didn't come to much. What did she expect? Every morning she polished the front of her house with a rag. In quick succession she was followed by the mothers of sturdy daughters from properties surrounding Holland's, inviting him to their homesteads facing north, where heaps of mutton were served. These were kitchen meals on pine scrubbed to a lung colour, the kitchens dominated by the flame-leaking mass of black stove; other houses employed the papered dining-room, the oakish-looking table, pieces of silver, crystal and Spode – a purple husband looking like death at the head. And the mothers and daughters watched with interest as this complete stranger in their midst took the food in by his exceptionally wide mouth, mopped up with his hunk of white bread. He nodded in appreciation. He dropped his aitches, which was a relief.

Afterwards he took out his handkerchief and wiped his hands, so to these mothers and daughters it was like a magician offering one of his khaki paddocks as an example, before whipping it away, leaving nothing.

Almost five months had passed; on a Monday morning Holland was seen at the railway station. The others standing about gave the country-nod, assuming he was there like them to collect machinery parts ordered from Sydney.

Holland took a cigarette.

The heavy rails went away parallel to the platform on the regularly spaced sleepers darkened by shadow and grease, and darkened further as they went away into the sunlight, the rails converging with a silver wobble in bushes, bend and mid-morning haze.

The train was late.

Those darkened sleepers which cushioned the tremendous travelling weight of trains: they had been axed from the forests of Grey Ironbark (*E. paniculata*) around hilly Bunyah, a few hours to the east. The same dark eucalypts felled by the same axemen filled export contracts for the expansion of steam across China, India, British Africa. Most of the sleepers for the Trans-Siberian railway were cut from the forests around Bunyah, and so – here's poetic justice – carried the weight of thousands of Russians, transported to isolation and worse. Truly, Grey Ironbark is one of the hardest woods available to man.

Faint whistle and smoke. The rails began their knuckle-cracking. The train appeared, grew, and eventually came to rest alongside the platform, letting out a series of sighs like an exhausted black dog, dribbling, its paws outstretched. For a moment people were too occupied to notice Holland.

Holland tilted his bare head down to a small girl in a blue dress. As they left the station he was seen taking her small wicker case and doing his best to talk. She was looking up at him.

Soon after, women came out in the sunlight on the street and appeared to bump into each other. They joined at the hem and elbow. The news quickly jumped the long distances out of town, and from there spread in different directions, entering the houses Holland had sat down and eaten in, the way a fire leaps over fences, roads, bare paddocks and rivers, depositing smaller, always slightly different, versions of itself.

She was his daughter. He could do anything he liked

with her. Yes; but weeks passed before he brought her into town. "Acclimatising" was very much on his mind.

The women wanted to see her. They wanted to see the two of them together. Some wondered if he'd be stern with her; the various degrees of. Instead Holland appeared unusually stiff, at the same time, casual.

Traces of him showed around the child's eyes and jaw. There was the same two-stage smile, and the same frown when answering a question. To the town women she was perfectly polite.

She was called Ellen.

Holland had met and married a river woman from outside Waikerie, on the Murray, in South Australia; Ellen never tired of hearing the story.

Her father had placed one of those matrimonial advertisements.

"What's wrong with that? It has a high curiosity value for both parties. You never know what's going to come up. That's what I'm going to do when you're old enough. I'll write the advertisement myself. I'll try to list your most attractive features, if I can think of any. We'll probably have to advertise in Scotland and Venezuela."

It is still the custom for certain rural newspapers to run these advertisements, handy for the man who simply hasn't got around to finding himself a suitable woman, or one who's been on the move, doing seasonal work. It's a custom well and truly established in other places, such as Nigeria, where men are given the names of flowers, and in India, one newspaper especially, published in New Delhi, is read avidly just for these advertisements artfully penned and placed from all corners of the subcontinent. There it's a convenient service for marriages arranged by others, when it becomes necessary to cast a wider net.

Worth mentioning in this context. In circular New Delhi, wherever the eye turns, even as a bride tilts her cloudy mirror-ring to glimpse for the first time the face with pencil-moustache of her arranged-by-others husband, it invariably picks up the Blue Gum (*E. globulus*) – they're all over the place; just as the tall fast-growing *E. kirtoni*, common name Half Mahogany, has virtually taken over the dusty city of Lucknow.

Of the three replies to Holland's one-liner clearly the most promising was the childish rounded hand on ruled paper. Some suggestion here about being a fresh widow: hers was another man who'd ended up headfirst in the river, still in his boots.

She was one of seven or eight. Holland saw bodies draped everywhere, pale sisters, transfixed by lines of piercing light, as if the tin shack had been shot up with bullet holes.

"I introduced myself," Holland explained. "And your mother went very quiet. She hardly opened her mouth. She must have realised what she'd let herself in for. Now there I was, standing in front of her. Maybe she took one look at my mug and wanted to run a mile?" Daughter smiled. "A very, very nice woman. I had a lot of time for your mother."

Sometimes a sister sat alongside and without a word began brushing the eldest sister's hair. It was straw-blonde; the others were dark. The kitchen table had its legs standing in jam-tins of kero. The father would come in and go out. He hardly registered Holland's presence. No sign of the mother. Holland presented an axe and a blanket, as if they were Red Indians.

At last he carried her back to Sydney.

There in his rooms, which was more or less within his world, she appeared plump, or (put it this way) softer than he imagined, and glowed, as if dusted with flour. And she busied herself. Casually she introduced a different order. Unpinned, her hair fell like a sudden dumping of sand and rhythmically she brushed it, a religious habit in front of the mirror. Amazing was her faith in him: how she allowed him to enter. His hands felt clumsy and coarse, as did sometimes his words. Here was someone who listened to him.

What happened next began as a joke. On the spur of the moment he took out, with some difficulty, insurance against his river woman delivering twins. He was challenging Nature. It was also his way of celebrating. The actuaries calculated tremendous odds; Holland immediately increased the policy. He waved the ye olde certificate with its phoney red seal in front of his friends. Those were the days he was drinking.

"I'd emptied my pockets, every spare zac I had."

Ellen had little interest in the financial side.

"You were the first-born," he nodded. "We named you Ellen. I mean, that was your mother's preference – Ellen. Your brother lived just a few days. Something broke in your mother. No one has ever seen anyone cry as much, I'm willing to bet. The top of your head, here, was always wet. And blood, a lot of blood. She just lay there crying, you know, softly. She couldn't stop. She grew weak with it. As I watched, her life seemed to leak away. There was nothing I could do. I'd hardly even got to know her. I don't know how it happened.

"And you, the picture of health and the fat cheque arriving soon afterwards. I should have been throwing my hat up in the air. I'd never seen so much money, so many noughts. I had all this dough on a piece of paper in the back of my trousers for a month or more before I had the stomach to march into a bank with it. And so, here we are. There's a fine view from the verandah. At least I've got some say in that. And look at you. Already you're the prettiest doll for a hundred miles."

And Ellen never tired of hearing the story, and asking questions, often the same questions, about her mother. Often in the retelling Holland would stop and say, "Come over here and give your father a big kiss."

2

Eximia

SOME PEOPLE, SOME nations, are permanently in
shade. Some people cast a shadow. Lengths of elongated
darkness precede them, even in church or when the sun is
in, as they say, mopped up by the dirty cloth of the clouds.
A puddle of dark forms around their feet. It's very *pine-like*.
The pine and darkness are one. Eucalypts are unusual in
this respect: set pendulously their leaves allow see-through
foliage which in turn produces a frail patterned sort of
shade, if at all. Clarity, lack of darkness – these might be
called "eucalyptus qualities".

Anyway, don't you think the compliant pine is associated
with numbers, geometry, the majority, whereas the eucalypt
stands apart, solitary, essentially undemocratic?

The gum tree has a pale ragged beauty. A single
specimen can dominate an entire Australian hill. It's an
egotistical tree. Standing apart it draws attention to itself
and soaks up moisture and all signs of life, such as harmless
weeds and grass, for a radius beyond its roots, at the same
time giving precious little in the way of shade.

It is trees which compose a landscape.

A long time passed before Holland could accept the idea

(rather than the fact) that the land he was standing on, including every lump of quartz and broken stick and tuft of dry grass, every tree upright and growing or fallen grey, belonged to him, was his. Sometimes then it felt as if even the weather belonged to him.

In a rush of keenness Holland decided he wanted to know everything, beginning with the names of things – the birds and the rocks, above all, the trees. Almost smiling and with a certain blank politeness the town people could not always come up with the answers; Holland ordered a number of reference books from Sydney.

By the time Ellen arrived in her blue-check dress Holland had planted a few eucalypts, and often she would accompany her father with a bucket and yellow spade, squatting alongside as he planted more.

So she, Ellen, was sowing the seeds of her own future.

The first eucalypt – if it's possible to be precise about a passion – is the one closest to the front of the house. Positioned off-centre it breaks the accelerating horizontality of the front verandah, and from most angles happens to obscure the window of the daughter's bedroom.

Holland could have put in any tree under the sun, a creepy pine, for example, with its sycophantic shadow (an Umbrella Pine? a Norfolk?), or else an acacia, the dreariest of all trees; a loquat would have been the sentimental local favourite. And if he was especially attracted to eucalypts, because they were native so-called, or solitary or whatever, plenty of different seedlings were commercially available in rusty tins, even in those days.

Holland planted a Yellow Bloodwood (*E. eximia*).

Here we have a tree so sensitive to frosts it sticks close to the coast, within cooee of Sydney. Holland's first attempt quickly died. With peculiar stubbornness he planted others, and nursed the last remaining plant, a weedy-looking thing. Every day he forked the earth, and gave it a drink from a cup, distributed bits of sheep manure, and at night threw up an anti-frost barricade of tin and hessian. It grew and thrived. There it stands now.

Unusual for a eucalypt the Yellow Bloodwood has a shivering canopy of leaves almost touching the ground, like an errant oak. The botanical journals have this to say: "The specific name is taken from the English adjective *eximious*, in the sense that the tree in flower is extraordinary." Late spring the flowers put on their show. It is as if someone has merrily chucked handfuls of dirty snow into the military-green leaves. Dirty snow – so far inland? Colour of beer froth. Make that a blonde's hair. Perpetually oozing red gum is the "blood" in the rest of the name.

As she grew older Ellen wanted to know still more about her invisible mother. The sophistication of Ellen's expectations, her impatience with his replies, puzzled her father.

A photograph might have eased the pressure. But apparently no such point of reference existed – although Holland's wife had grown up in the very midst of a national outbreak of black-and-white as well as brown photography, the flowering of the gawky pose. (The boredom of picnics caught, black sheep there pulling faces, the country cousin in the old teapot pose, babies grimacing in prams like angry motorcyclists. God knows, a long list of the regulation snaps could be made, along with a disgusted footnote on the unreliability of the locally made photo-corners ...) From the moment the shutter clicks, future reactions of shock-horror, pity and surprise are stored in silver and gelatin. Photography is the art of comparison. Anyone can take a photograph. The "art" has already been composed by the subject itself, even when it's a brick wall – really, the word "art" here is an amazing pretension, since it is merely a description of feet placement, whether the photographer aims for the poetics of shadow, the curious subject or juxtaposition, the concentration of austerity, or merely the decency of the ordinary mugshot.

"They could hardly afford a loaf of bread," Holland explained, "let alone a box camera. They had sores, and no shoes. I think their place had a dirt floor."

As well, the great river was known to spill over every set number of years and carry away the most intimate possessions of a person.

Whatever the reason, Ellen was left feeling incomplete, conscious of a missing element.

Holland did his best. To picture Ellen's mother he first had to smooth away the blood thinned with the dripping tears which had seeped into her dress, dissolved her shape, that is, those hips, wrists, breasts, mouth with expression, her voice – not that she was one of the world's great talkers.

But then he saw the woman he hardly knew had haemorrhaged gentleness, whether breathing at his side or sitting in a kitchen chair, an abundance of gentleness, *over-flowing*, so much gentleness and with it serenity, he had trouble realising her true centre. And as time passed this too began to fade.

He hadn't told Ellen about her grandfather. Holland wasn't sure what to say about him. Quite a scenario on the outskirts of Waikerie: father, seven or eight daughters growing up inside an oven, mother nowhere to be seen, drowsy brown river slow-flowing in sunlight. Even though Holland had been about to stroll away with his eldest daughter, and so was there most days with his hair Brylcreemed and parted, the father took little notice of him. Loose-limbed, a wreck, a pisspot; by the popular American handbooks on the family, strong on statistics, he was a total disappointment, a really poor low-grade example of what a father should be.

What exactly is a father to a daughter?

The father is a man, yet to the daughter he is not. Wherever she goes he is behind or alongside at an angle, her often clumsy shadow. She'll never shake him off. The father has the advantage of the older man. He is solid; at arm's length; at the same time, distant: a blurry authority, always with the promise of softening. And this particular father in the torn singlet, this black spot on the statistical curve, had a mermaid tattooed on the wrist (a long way from the sea) whose perspiring breasts and fishy hips he liked to wriggle for his many daughters by opening and closing his fist. Talk about mixed signals: he was caught doing it at the funeral.

Holland's wife had told about the games they played on the river bank, she and her many sisters.

All shrieks and plaits and grazed knees they singled out a tree and took turns to embrace it, whispering against the trunk. It felt iron-hard, though alive, like the tremendous neck of a horse. According to this game any sister whose fingertips met around the trunk would become pregnant. By "pregnant" they meant marriage; they were only girls.

One of these sisters, young and fairly fat, was standing by the tree on a hot afternoon when she was made pregnant. It was a thudding-in, the way countrymen using their strength grapple with a fresh ironbark fencing post. That was the way it happened. Half on the land, half in midair. She was barely sixteen. A few months later everybody knew.

Holland's mail-order bride led him to the water and pointed to the lingam tree. Holland almost burst out laughing at its bedraggled ordinariness, its helpfully small circumference. (A young Swamp Gum – its leery specific name, *Eucalyptus ovata*.) Wrapping his bare arms around the trunk Holland shook hands with himself, and to underline the ease said, "Pleased to meetya." She looked on with an attentive slight smile.

"I knew then she was going to give me the nod. I'd say she'd decided there and then. Your mother always liked a joke."

Her gentleness and serenity – it could have been indifference. He was never sure.

It was near the same tree on one other afternoon that something had leaked into her eye, so to speak; her head jerked, her fingers went up and twisted her lips. Other times she'd seen sheep and cows made amphibious, and once a horse, their bellies blown up to billy-o. Never the body of a man in a check shirt coming by slowly with the current, face-down.

As she searched for a long branch or something she made whimpering sounds.

Her father grabbed her from behind: his pet mermaid would have flexed into a belly dance. Not far upstream was the spot he kept his beer cool, submerged in a wheat bag to the depth of an elbow. Now he was digging into her shoulders.

"Let him be, poor sap. He'll get snagged soon enough. Stop your blubbering, you hear?"

Even as he spoke the body stopped, the river swirled and built up against it. The face tilted towards them. But she knew anyway it was the skinny fruit-picker who'd been seen with her sister.

She wondered if she could reach out with a stick. The body though swung with the current and got moving again. Eventually it came to rest near the town bridge, jammed in the fork of a tree, along with a bucket and other rubbish. What a way to end: amongst things of exceptional ordinariness.

For days their sister swollen to mother-of-pearl wouldn't speak to anyone. Then she was found eating handfuls of dirt, which their father saw as proof, if further proof was needed, of an altogether different sort of deficiency – not even his savage elbow could stop her.

Elsewhere in history virgins have imagined themselves pregnant; many stories are told of them. But she felt clumsy in her heaviness. She was two and wanted to be back to one; or at least separate from the extra living heaviness within, bearing down at several points. Fluid was pulling her earthwards: a sponge heavy with liquid. Even her pretty feet had swollen. She lost count of the days. She was too young. For no other reason she answered one weekend – there was nothing else to do – Holland's advertisement and became engrossed in an earnest correspondence. Somehow she knew the words "young widow" were red rag to a long-distant man, even if she wasn't exactly, not officially. With her eldest sister helping she replied to his suggestion of an exchange of photographs: "Come and see for yourself!"

And there he was a few days later, standing in the door-way, not really expected. No one knew which way to turn.

The swollen and smeared one doing her best to merge into the flowers and broken springs of the sofa hissed, "I'm not talking to him, you have to, go on."

She and the others unravelled into the shadows, tittering. The eldest was left then to say something, or at least sit there.

From the doorway Holland could see her clearly, whereas his face was draped in shadow. By not moving she appeared to be offering herself. Later she wondered if she had decided there and then.

That was how it happened. Holland had not taken his eyes off her. And she found herself listening to what he was saying. After a while she began answering, eventually raising her arm slightly, which drew attention to her extraordinary hair.

3

Australiana

SOME DESCRIPTION OF landscape is necessary.

At the same time (be assured) strenuous efforts will be made to avoid the rusty traps set by ideas of a National Landscape, which is of course an interior landscape, fitted out with blue sky and the obligatory tremendous gum tree, perhaps some merinos chewing on the bleached-out grass in the foreground, the kind of landscape seen during home-sickness and in full colour on suburban butchers' calendars handed out with the sausages at Christmas ("Pleased to meet, meat to please" etc.). Every country has its own land-scape which deposits itself in layers on the consciousness of its citizens, thereby cancelling the exclusive claims made by all other national landscapes. Furthermore, so many eucalypts have been exported to different countries in the world, where they've grown into sturdy see-through trees, and infected the purity of these landscapes. Summer views of Italy, Portugal, Northern India, California, to take obvious examples, can appear at first glance as classic Australian landscapes – until the eucalypts begin to look slightly out of place, like giraffes in Scotland or Tasmania.

A few descriptive passages then of Holland's property,

west of Sydney, which receives rain and dry winds at certain times of the year.

Actually the trouble with our National Landscape is that it produced a certain type of behaviour which has been given shape in story-telling, all those laconic hard-luck stories, as many as there are burrs on the backs of sheep, and just as difficult to remove. Yes, yes: there's nothing more dispiriting, *déjà vu*, than to come across another story of disappointment set in the Australian backblocks. And now, towards the end of the century, just when you might think they have reduced to a trickle, the same kind of pale brown story has appeared in the cities, in disguise! Figures move about between asphalt and engines, displaying a familiar solemn sentimentality; sometimes it's dressed up in a poetic mist, a pleasure to read: stories such as the ex-POW with heart of gold, or else we have lovesick young women by the harbour, others opining on verandahs in the mountains, and if there are painters in stories naturally they are made to live in the purity of squalor . . . At regular intervals the stubborn maleness of an unsuspecting father is put under the inner-city microscope, so to speak, the old peeling away of layers. Not to mention the many hundreds of stories told in the confessional first person singular, with still more to come. A kind of applied psychology has taken over story-telling, coating it and obscuring the core.

What is frail falls away; stories that take root become like *things*, misshapen things with an illogical core, which pass through many hands without wearing out or falling to pieces, remaining in essence the same, adjusting here and there at the edges, nothing more, as families or forests reproduce ever-changing appearances of themselves; the geology of fable. In Alexandria, eucalypts were grown in front of houses to ward off evil spirits, including fatal diseases.

From his front verandah Holland's land went away to the right in the direction of the town.

It was the most visible unbroken stretch, although it ended in a purplish blur, and a faint glitter as if someone there was flashing a mirror – a small mystery which Holland would never solve. Along one side a tree line stood up like a haircut, where Holland occasionally emerged, pale flesh against grey wash. The land then sloped down plump and smooth, as if patted unevenly by hand, worn in patches to river frontage. It rose and fell along the floor, though less so, broken by outcrops of rock. The rabbits had left erosions of miniature ravines. There were snakes. River Red Gums hogged all the water in their usual dishevelled manner, resistant to the axe and just about everything else; there are many stories about their hardness. Following the river Holland trod carefully over the rotting elbows of wood, black mud, then stooped, to reach all corners. And large dark birds floated overhead, rags torn from the dead anywhere else, except the air was clear, the sky wide open; for a moment anything felt possible here.

People on the surrounding properties were called Lomax, Cork, Cronin, Kearney, Gulley, even a Stain (old Les) and the Sprunt sisters; the Sheldrakes, the Traill, Wood and Kelly families were further afield. One man out there changed his surname to that of his best friend, who was killed under a horse. No greater love hath one man . . . In town there was a Long and a Short (Les again); Manifold lived there; Mr Brian Brain ran the one and only hotel with a buck-toothed wife. The visiting signwriter who appeared every third year on the dot, looking more like a plumber in his green vibrating truck, to touch up the serifs on the shopfronts, was called Zoellner, but unfortunately he doesn't count. For these names had roots going way back, bog-Irish, Yorkshire, bony Scot. Christian names followed the crooked streets of Sydney: Clarence, Phil, George, Bert, Beth and a Gregory. No one had come across a Holland before.

Usually Holland was seen at mid-distance poking around in one of his paddocks. People on the road to town would say, "Behind that Stringybark, look." Or, "One of these days I'm going to buy him a hat." And men would run their eyes over the place to spot his daughter.

Holland's father had been a baker in Tasmania; a little chap, gold fillings. More or less a convert to Methodism he could hardly wait for the next day to begin. Behind the counter of the town's cakeshop was a thin girl with a very small mouth. She gave attentive encouragement to his ideas and schemes for the near future, mostly in the field of buns, some containing hidden almonds – just a thought.

Soon after, she made it clear they should move – and as far away as possible from the village split by the main road. "I don't see myself as an island person," she explained.

As a consequence, Holland was born in Sydney, in the suburb called Haberfield. Even today the feeling remains in Haberfield of space beginning to spread and open in every direction.

Here Holland's parents set up a little business making boiled lollies in the shed in the backyard. Holland grew up with the treacly smell of over-heated sugar, and a mother with sticky hands, which could help explain why for the rest of his life he never allowed, under any circumstances, sugar in his tea, and resisted for so long before finally planting, though out of sight from the house, a Sugar Gum (*E. cladocalyx*), when everybody knows the Sugar Gum is central to understanding eucalypts, at least visually.

Black Peppermints with a zebra stripe became the Hollands' speciality, wrapped with (mother's idea) a deluxe twist of cellophane. In the afternoons Holland's father changed his shirt and made deliveries throughout the suburbs.

For a time everybody in Sydney seemed to be ruining their good teeth sucking on a Black Peppermint made in the shed in the Haberfield backyard. Printers, bank managers, insurance agents, suppliers of fancy cardboard boxes, hopeful distributors and health inspectors all made their way to the source, schoolchildren too, and none left without a small bag of Black Peppermints.

A builder, who happened to be the local mayor, was drawn to the humid feminine sweetness of the shed, the concrete path to the shed. He had windswept ginger hairs on his hands. One afternoon Holland glimpsed in a corner his mother's floury nakedness, circular and fluid, her mouth angled, the mayor's bare shoulders overlapping.

During it all Holland's father saw no reason to stop smiling; in his sleep he held a gold smile at the ceiling. Everything before him, including strange feelings and warnings, had equal value. And instead of caressing him with wellbeing the perpetual smiling left him in the opposite position: his face prematurely worn, like a jockey's after straining too long to keep under the weight. The morning he left with his suitcase his mouth was clenched into the same smile of optimism or equality, although the tan comb bravely clipped to his shirt pocket alongside the ballpoint suggested a different story.

The builder now occupied one end of the kitchen table, where he signed his papers and worked the telephone; pencil stubs and receipt books and samples of veneers and tiles piled everywhere.

Aside from building entire streets of red-brick houses, as well as shopfronts, garages, motels and long orange-brick walls, he had his mayoral duties, which meant dressing up in robes, and attending all kinds of functions.

And because he was a successful builder, or was a mayor, or perhaps because he was a man, he developed a strong belief in patriotism; he even tinkered with the idea of turning out flagpoles and selling them more or less at cost. He had one made up and placed in the front yard at Haberfield, the only flagpole for miles; but there in the side street our national flag hardly stirred, occasionally catching the land breezes at night, when nobody could see it.

He couldn't keep his fingers still, even when talking on the telephone. A businessman, he explained to the boy, is simply shorthand for *busyman*.

"If you're not doing anything, wear these in for me."

A shoebox landed at Holland's feet. Holland's first thought was whether he'd fit into his stepfather's shoes.

"If my feet are killing me, I'm not doing myself any favours. You understand? You would not believe how many functions I've got on my plate."

The businessman subdivides the world into manageable units, some as small as a split second. It becomes all-absorbing managing the units, fulfilling the possibilities within them. Success is based on a constant reference to scepticism; that's right, deploying scepticism in a truly positive sense, which is why business is not a difficult calling for men. Hardly any time is left for ordinary things. For a spec-builder who doubled as a mayor even buying clothes was a problem. He got around it by every few years buying off the rack six of everything – six of those plain white shirts, the diamond-patterned socks, black lace-up shoes with toecaps.

To break in the shoes Holland numbered the soles. He then tried on the first pair and squeaked about the house. He did the same with the second pair, before retreating to the comfort of his own shoes, and so on. In the third week he ventured out onto the street – until, in less than a month, he handed all six pairs back to his impatient stepfather, ready to wear.

Any mention of this episode was enough for Ellen to send a hand flying to her mouth. "How could you do it? Why couldn't he do it for himself?"

"I got paid," Holland said.

"It's awful, it's one of the most awful things I've ever heard. I hope I never have a stepfather."

Holland looked interested. A daughter indignant on his behalf was pleasing, even if it was well over the top. "Until you bring it up I don't give it a moment's thought," he shrugged. "It's a mildly interesting story among dozens, if you see what I mean."

Still, the saga of the shoes was the early sign of his instinct for completeness, classification, order; his way of encompassing to all corners a given subject or situation, and the enjoyment of the absorption it brought!

She always liked it when he became absorbed; but you never knew where it would end. Somehow their different reactions to the story of the shoes represented something of the separation of father and daughter, even though they felt as one, and in this she saw the uncertain distance which apparently existed between her and all other men: not distance so much as a shelf at her elbow, with a high right-angled edge.

From the property Holland displayed a certain caution towards the surrounding rural values, evident too in the nearby town. Early on he had packed his daughter off to the nuns in Sydney, until – for no apparent reason – abruptly bringing her back. At least in Sydney she learned to sew and swim and to wear gloves. In the dormitory she developed the eager way of talking, between girlfriends, and the uses of silence; on weekends at distant relations' Ellen while scraping vegetables liked to overhear the stories told by men, and she could watch as lipstick was carefully applied. On the property she roamed about wild. He seemed to allow it. Then she became quiet: in her teens. Almost unconsciously, he supervised her movements; it felt like the bestowing of protection. God knows, he didn't want

31

his daughter bolting off to the shadowy Odeon in town, where the stammering projector drowned out a good 70 per cent of the words, and then sliding about on the seats of the fluorescent milk bar, like others her age.

If these were restrictions, they didn't trouble Ellen.

Around this time she stopped going about the house naked, though her father continued the habit in the corridor to the bathroom, all elbows and red knees, and in a similar cantilevered action most days of the year jumped into the river with swinging cock, something farmers never do, and floated in the brown water towards the suspension bridge, gazing up at the clouds: one minute brain-shaped, framed by boughs, before stretching into the windswept head of a sage or a scientist – Albert Einstein, say.

There was something unpleasantly ravenous about Holland's naked rush and the complete obliviousness of his splashings. If Ellen thought as much she didn't say. Almost overnight she had become beautiful. She had grown from a small darting-about figure to a gliding, drifting, fuller one. It was a speckled beauty. She was so covered in small brown-black moles she attracted men, every sort of man. These few too many birthmarks of the first-born tipped the balance on her face and throat: men felt free to wander with their eyes all over, across the pale spaces and back again to the factual dots, the way a full stop brings to a halt a meandering sentence. And she allowed it, her face was unresisting; she didn't seem to notice them. So the men felt unstoppable, going from one point to the next, even under her chin and back to the one touching her top lip, and it was as if they were running with their eyes over every part of her nakedness.

Word of Ellen spread gradually from the town and across the paddocks and hills; she was unzipped by the railway line to other country towns; to the suburbs of Sydney; faint aftershocks reaching distant capitals of other states and other countries. And the idea of her beauty grew with its scarcity value. The face and limbs with the birthmarks and everything else generally remained on the other side of the river, out of reach, as it were, through the trees. And as her speckled beauty became legendary the suspicion grew the father wanted it hidden.

A paragraph is not so different from a paddock – similar shape, similar function. And here's a connection worth pondering: these days, as paddocks are becoming larger, the corresponding shift in the cities where the serious printing's done is for paragraphs smaller. A succession of small paddocks can be as irritating as long ones wearisome. The single-idea paragraph which crowds the newspapers is a difficulty. Newspaper writers spend their lives trailing after people above the ordinary in some way or other – the human equivalents to earthquakes, train crashes, rivers in flood – and write small paragraphs about them, when everybody knows that a brief rectangular view is not enough. The people written about in newspapers have already made something visible of their lives, large or small, brief or lasting, which is surely why journalists take an interest out of all proportion in newspaper proprietors: for here is one of us, or almost, who is larger than life. Holland too would attract journalists, some with the bedraggled photographer in tow from the Sydney broadsheets. These days it's common to trudge (as the reporters were forced to do) across a paddock that seems to go on forever and ever, amen. Other paddocks may be congested, untidy, restricting movement. It's just as easy these days to get clogged up or tripped in the middle of a paragraph! As in a paddock it is sometimes necessary to retrace our steps. Easy to lose heart, lose your way. In these and other situations the impulse is to take the short cut. "A problem paddock" – there's a common description. Words, yakety-yak, are spoken within the paddock (paragraph). The rectangle is a sign of civilisation: Europe from the air. Civilisation? A paragraph begins as a rectangle and by chance may finish up a square. Who was it said the square doesn't exist in nature? A paddock has an alteration in the fencing for the point of entry, just as a paragraph has an indentation to encourage entry. A paddock too is littered with nouns and Latin in italics, even what appears to be a bare paddock. When Holland began planting the trees it was casually, no apparent design.

A paragraph is supposed to fence off wandering thoughts.

4

Diversifolia

THE WORD *eucalypt* is from the Greek, "well" and "covered". It describes something peculiar to the genus. Until they open, ready for fertilisation, the eucalypt's buds are covered by an operculum, in effect putting a lid on the reproductive organs.

It is all very prudish. At the same time – and here we find paradox is a leading characteristic of the eucalypt – the surrounding leaves are almost promiscuous in their flaunting of different thicknesses, shapes, colours and shine: "fixed irregularity" is botany's way of putting it. One or two species even sport variegated leaves. Strangely with eucalypts, the higher on the tree the smaller the leaf. Another paradox: the largest eucalypts have the smallest flowers.

The barks come in a bewildering range of textures and colours and so on, unusual for one genus, and often end up as final arbiters in the game of identification.

There is still learned debate over the precise number of eucalypts. It's well into the hundreds, but the figure keeps changing. At regular intervals there's a career move from an institutional dark corner somewhere to reduce the total. Recently it has been suggested the Ghost Gum, which has long stood as the archetypal eucalypt, is *not* a eucalypt at all, but a member of the "Corymbia family". The new name, if you don't mind, would be *Corymbia aparrarinja*. Isn't that a marriage of the Mafia and the Aboriginal? A good many people are trying to come to terms with this. A young nation has shallow roots and the slightest disturbance can throw out the equilibrium, patriotically speaking. Nationalism is nothing less than clutching at straws. It can only be hoped the ruling on the Ghost Gum will be revised again, or at least delayed. On the other hand, the invisible eucalypt, known by hearsay as *E. rameliana*, though never actually seen by anybody of authority, at last had a confirmed sighting in 1992 in the waterless wastes west of Uluru, so adding one to the eucalypt's grand total. Monsieur Ramel, by the way, was the man who introduced eucalypts to Algeria.

It is this chaotic diversity that has attracted men to the world of eucalypts. For here was a maze of tentative half-words and part-descriptions, constantly expanding and contracting, almost out of control – a world within the world, but too loosely contained. It cried out for a "system" of some kind, where order could be imposed on a region of nature's unruly endlessness.

This attempt to "humanise" nature by naming its parts has a long and distinguished history. Once a given subject is broken down into parts, each one identified, named and placed into groups – the periodic table, strata of minerals, weight divisions of prizefighters – the whole is given limits and becomes acceptable, or digestible, almost. It may as well be regarded as residual evidence of the oldest fear, the fear of the infinite. Anything to escape the darkness of the forest. Some men and women have been known to devote their lives to the study of nothing but the leaves of the euca-lypts and grow old without mastering the subject. In time they resemble those gentle maiden aunts who reveal on request tremendous genealogical knowledge, the Christian names and histories of the family's branches, who has been married to who and how many children, their names and illnesses, who died of what, and so forth; the history of hybrids.

The point is, in the world of trees, only the acacia has more species than the eucalyptus – but look at the acacia, a series of pathetic little bushes. Whenever on his property Holland saw clumps of wattle, as the acacia is called, he lost no time pulling them out by the roots.

The Black Peppermint on the slight slope between house and river was planted soon after Yellow Bloodwood. Accordingly it is engraved in Holland's pantheon, like the bevelled names in small towns of soldiers who led a charge against all the odds across no-man's-land. As he studied the botanical names and saw that Black Peppermint, a native of Tasmania, was also known on the mainland as *E. australiana*, the tree evidently began waving attention to itself as a sort of flagpole of the subconscious.

Of course, from any angle the Black Peppermint looks nothing like a flagpole (and Holland had no right to load a simple eucalypt with worthless associations).

It's not slender and certainly not whitewashed: see instead the one called Boongul or the Candlebark or the

Wallangarra White, splendid examples decorating Holland's land, not to mention the white-as-a-sheet Ghost Gum. In fact, the eucalypt's normally smooth lower trunk is obscured on the Black Peppermint by a mass of twigs and leaves, the way a beard rushes to the weak chin of a man, filings to a magnet.

The sight of *E. eximia* and *E. australiana* flourishing with their brave glossy little leaves must have heartened Holland. With no particular design he planted a few more.

Trees were better than nothing, instructed the eye; this wasn't the Sahara.

Even then (that is, from the very beginning) it never occurred to him to opt for *introduced species* – the oaks, willows, walnuts and what-have-you, the various shade-producing elms, cedars, the cypress of the Mediterranean, let alone the terminally gloomy pine – better left to be pulped into newsprint and the low-rent paper used these days in literary and philosophical works. His affinity with eucalypts was both vague and natural; and before long he was having slow-motion dreams about them. (There'll be no descriptions of Holland's tree-dreams here! They would only try the patience of the reader, or else encourage inter-pretation. In city life, forests figure in dreams, as well as flowers and teeth and noses in close-up, and the usual slow flying, floating and zooming in, whereas someone asleep in the country, where shadows are fewer, and greater space exists between objects and people . . .)

After a dozen or so plantings Holland stood back and saw he would have to add others here and there to avoid giving a false, lopsided look.

In this he followed the greatest painters and English landscape gardeners who struggled with the difficulty of reproducing the randomness of true harmony, demonstrated so casually in nature.

Of course, plenty of eucalypts were already growing on the property when Holland arrived. Not all had been ring-barked by the brothers. Red Stringybark and Red Ironbark were dotted about – these were native to the region; similarly, Yellow Box, the beekeepers' favourite – all over the place. Tumbledown Gums showed along the ridge, Scribbly Gums were on the flat, and Rose-of-the-West, which barely comes up to a man's head. A few Inland Red Box remained: farmers take the axe to them for fence posts. Other species were distributed by wind and chance, each different from the rest. Out of sight of the homestead, paddocks here and there contained unusual eucalypts in amongst the common local ones. Nobody knew how they got there. A rogue Mountain Ash reigned on the slope above the house, forcing a pregnancy on the fence. Easily the tallest tree in the district, it was the base for generations of wedgetails, crows and parrots, their constructions of aerial sticks like the shadowy congestions in a sieve. Not far from it was a stocky Tuart (*E. gomphocephala*). Again we have a tree rarely seen east of the Nullarbor. A seed must have dropped out of the sky or a man's trouser cuff. Something like that, Holland decided.

With a boiled egg and the standard textbooks in a knapsack Holland criss-crossed his land, absorbed in identifying each and every eucalypt. Often it was necessary to send specimens of fruit and leaves to a world authority in

Sydney, and seek a second opinion in other places. No one expert in eucalypts had all the answers. So pale and hyper-sensitive were these experts, relegated as they were to the backwaters of irrelevant institutions, they replied by return with a helpful vehemence, supplying far too much detail.

In those days Holland would listen with interest to anybody. He was leaving the hotel one morning when a man with a wrecked face took an Ancient Mariner hold on his elbow and raved about the advantages of the scientific windbreak, and the very same evening Holland heard on the radio the same thing explained in a sober, altogether more reasonable voice.

Parallel to one side of the house, he planted 110 seedlings in scientific formation. Chosen were species renowned as windbreaks: the fast-growing Steedman's Gum, and the Mugga Ironbark – its specific name *E. sideroxylon* points more to the blast furnace than to pretty flowers and leaves. In the midst of this elongated geometry Holland placed an intruder, a single Grey Ironbark. Only many years later would it begin to be visible, with consequences for Ellen almost too horrible to bear.

Blue Gum, Salmon Gum and others quickly followed. Blue Gum is the one below the house which appeared from some angles as a pin stuck in a woman's hat, awash in patriotic grasses – golden in summer. Holland set up a swing for Ellen on its lower branches. Here the land fell away and rose again in gentle waves. It was as bare and as dusty as shorn sheep, until rendered park-like by Holland's hand. The Blue Gum is easily recognisable. The name *E. globulus*, for the shape of its fruit, now describes the imperial distribution of this majestic tree: throughout the Mediterranean, whole forests in California and South Africa, and all states of Australia.

As for *E. salmonophloia*, Holland had given it prime location at the front gate.

Holland must have known it would stop the locals in their tracks. The Salmon Gum is normally found on the other side of the continent, near the goldfields of Western Australia. Salmon refers to the pinkish bark. Transplanted, the trunk of Holland's was powdery-smooth, more like a rubber-band; "the colour of a nun's belly", someone else would say.

Trees have followed the great migrations of the Irish, the Italians, the Jews, the Brits, the Greeks as they put down roots in foreign soil. The superimposition of different colours, shadows and water usage, as well as droppings of leaves, attracts misunderstandings and downright hostility – in Portugal the peasants have been ripping out young eucalypts – until the trees grow as part of the scenery, in front of which all cultures go through their motions.

On the flat ground alongside the river, species of smooth girth had been chosen to represent (so it seemed) the uniform stillness of a rubber plantation; and long rectangles of silverish light angled in through the round-trunk verticals like searchlights seeking a solitary escapee, catching only a few moths and carefree birds.

Ellen liked to run blindly into the centre of it all, until the silence replaced her footsteps, blanketing her eyes and mind with *Slow Inevitable Growth* and *Patience Forever* and *Nothing Is One*; and surrounded by the multiplications of impassive trunks of the same diameter and same grey-green smoothness she'd half-imagine herself lost, and losing all sense of direction would let out a feeble cry, little more than a squeak, which was really the thrill of knowing her father and the house were only a few minutes away. She did this the day she first menstruated; a celebration of growth and confusion. The pale red of her fingerprints she tested on a trunk was the only primary colour in the grove.

Remaining very still she noticed all manner of insects and little reptiles shifting about on uneven surfaces, while from a far distance the clip-clopping of a horse was her father's Kelly axe ring-barking a tree surplus to his requirements.

Stillness is beauty, always.

In our country a harmless tradition has been for the larger properties to lead the eye from the road up to the homestead via an avenue, a green artery of plane trees, or poplars that stand up like feathers. It depended on the history of the property and associated feelings of grandiloquence in the owners; how they saw themselves in the district.

After going through the available anthographies Holland selected eucalypts for density of foliage, each different but set to reach the same height.

Ellen helped by holding the surveyor's string.

"One fine day this is all going to be yours," Holland gave a violent twist on the post-hole digger.

As always her father spoke in brief assertions. Now a question seemed to lengthen his jaw, "Do you like the house, as a place?"

She thought of her bedroom with her things and the blue curtains, the verandahs, the warmth of the kitchen. There were many empty rooms. Some dolls she'd left in the tower she found faded when she returned months later. Now and then the idea of having a brother had an urgent appeal, though she wondered whether he'd let her follow him around. And he, this father-shape, could almost be a brother when – an example – he allowed her to laugh in his face the moment he began explaining yet again that foxes at night have mauve eyes, and spiders glitter on the earth like stars.

After the windbreak, the "rubber plantation" and the ornamental avenue, Holland turned his back on mass formations. From now on he concentrated on individual species, planted singly. Otherwise there was no plan behind his programme. Gradually he filled in the landscape. He slept for long periods. Days and weeks of inactivity were spent in bed, followed by intense activity. All along he avoided planting duplicates; and soon he ran into problems of supply. The more successful his program the more difficult it became to continue.

Many years were spent culling, reducing most species to a single healthy specimen.

At the same time he strengthened his lines of supply; it was necessary to go far beyond the state of New South Wales. Useful information came from the most unlikely sources. Holland's land was looking different and people began to look at him differently. When they listened they wore what may be called conservative grins. It was only natural the locals would be imprecise on the subject of eucalypts, and suffer appalling memory lapses, or casually mention something without realising its importance. Often while talking on the street Holland pulled out a scrap of paper and made a note; for example, the address of an obscure roadside nursery in the Northern Territory run by the second cousin of somebody's stepsister, a Latvian, who had every known Australian parrot in cages, and who had perfected the art of painting desert scenes of photographic precision on emu eggs. That was where Holland acquired the island-loving *E. nesophila*, which has the urn-shaped fruit, and the Rough-leaved Range Gum (*E. aspersa*), very rare, difficult to grow.

Every other week Holland was seen on the railway platform collecting seedlings wrapped in damp hessian, and one of the Sprunt sisters complained to anyone who'd listen that the dusty trucks delivering still more specimens were keeping her awake at night. The postmistress too reported a steady flow of seeds rustling around in manila envelopes, as well as monthly journals, and invoices decorated with sprigs.

On days when Holland secured an especially rare specimen he felt like a pearl-diver who has burst to the surface, holding up a treasure. Certain eucalypts were rare because they rarely took root beyond a narrow radius. They were sensitive to drainage, lime in the soil, degrees of frost, elevation, rainfall and God knows what. Some stubbornly refused to grow in the month of March, others the week after Christmas. One tree would thrive in the shade of another; another would not. They were hypochondriacs, demanding esoteric manures and watering by hand.

How he managed to cultivate to healthy size a Darwin Woollybutt (*E. miniata*), or those born in sandy deserts, is a mystery. The Silvertop Stringybark (*E. laevopinea*) requires 1000mm rainfall every year, and the Snow Gum, its name proclaims, thrives on altitude, sleet and ice. Somehow he had eucalypts coming forth on ordinary ground when normally they demanded clay, flat marsh or granite. After many false starts he encouraged the little Yellowtop Ash, so called, to poke out of some rocks. And so on.

This vast labour with axe, crowbar and bucket, and the hatless traversing of paddocks gave him coarse hands and split fingernails, lined his face and made it brown; though as he came forward on the main street there was no doubt he still had trace elements of delicacy, of pastry, the only son of a disappointed baker.

Did he eventually manage to have growing on his property every known eucalypt? What was he going to do next? With his daughter, Ellen, he'd always encouraged questions; but she didn't seem interested. He was always waiting. The father is always waiting for the daughter. If only she had asked he would have told her everything he knew. He was a world authority in a narrow field. It was not that he wanted to give out bits and pieces of knowledge, he wanted to share his interest. Early on she'd been his helper. Together they planted well over a hundred trees, until she seemed to lose interest.

It was virtually an outdoor museum of trees. A person could wander amongst the many different species and pick up all kinds of information, at the same time be enthralled, in some cases rendered speechless, by the clear examples of beauty. The diversity of the eucalypts itself was an education. At the slightest movement of the head there was always another eucalypt of different height, foliage and pattern of bark, and there was the weird-looking homestead as well, impressive in its dark imbalance, and glimpsed at a window or in a cotton dress at the middle distance, with an elbow welded to a tree, his daughter.

Holland had toyed with the idea of fitting labels to the trees.

Eventually he had them made up by the same firm that supplied the Royal Botanic Gardens in Sydney, the common and specific names neatly engraved on rectangles of weather-proof aluminium, about hand-size. A bright young chap had delivered them personally – a partner in the firm. Together they checked them over on the verandah, while talking about this and that. It took them hours. When Ellen came out with tea on a tray they were so engrossed all she could see was the stranger's neck, and Holland didn't introduce her. Later Holland would leave the names piled in the corner of his office which doubled as his bedroom. After all, by then he could identify each and every eucalypt, almost without looking.

A few notes, nothing definite, on *feminine beauty*. Briefly, and in a timid, earnest voice. Of course; why not? The idea of Ellen's beauty had travelled long distances (was said to have crossed two oceans) and in the process inscribed a small legend.

Here it's worth noting that beauty composed of porcelain niceness produces a weaker response in men than a "beauty" that appears more aware of itself. Smoothness, niceness – they're the kiss of death. In the male they activate obscure notions of the Mother! And – sexually speaking – who wants that? Whereas if the main component in beauty is a certain dissatisfaction or bad temper, it banishes in men all associations with the mother and so allows an immediate, unencumbered attraction across a broad front.

All this was multiplied in Ellen by another factor.

In the brief time when women wore little hats with veils screening their faces, like delicately crumpled graph paper, the little squares filled in here and there gave the face a random distribution of oriental birthmarks and moles. And Ellen's speckled beauty resembled this veiled effect – protected, veiled, even in close-up; a kind of provocative, insincere modesty.

In order to survive she grew aloof, avoiding the eyes of men in town.

The first man who saw Ellen naked was the only son of a local tractor dealer, Molloy. He was popular, a strong footballer. His father had recently given him a motorbike with an iridescent petrol tank.

There was that dirt road alongside Holland's property: it had no other function but to go on towards town, while its twin, the similar-coloured river, took a sluggish lunge away from the road, establishing on the distant curve a density of River Red Gums which never failed to attract the eye of sportsmen, even if to reach it meant crawling on all fours through the undergrowth. There was a sandy pool on the curve, concealed by overhanging branches which mottled and browned the water to tortoiseshell.

On a very hot day Ellen splashed in . . . came up with both hands sweeping hair back from her eyes. For a while she lay on her back, eyes closed; and in the pale combination of flesh and water, which can both be taken to the lips or penetrated by a hand, three dark areas beckoned.

When she stood in the shallows her breasts swung a little.

On both sides the fat gums appeared as an entourage of sturdy older women, raising their skirts above their knees, about to wade into the water.

Squatting, Ellen began pissing.

Young Molloy was behind a tree. To see better he took the squatting position too. A fly began crawling towards his nose. Eventually he lowered his eyes – to contemplate the future?

Accelerating away with legs splayed around the engine, increasingly slit-eyed, watery, he began yelling out at what had been granted to him. Without much warning he felt it all slip on the dirt from under him, the engine spun, and he yawned as he was met in the face by the barbed wire, which tore off most of his nose.

As owner of the fence Holland was an early visitor.

"He sure was feeling pretty sorry for himself," Holland told Ellen. "Both parents were there, no hard feelings about our fence. They are just pleased to still have him. It's all they could talk about. I suppose he's still alive, but it's not going to be much of a life. Milking cows is all he'll be good for."

He lost the sight of one eye, quickly followed by the other.

Ellen had been told about his healthy good looks. It was said in town he had a wild streak.

"I don't want to see you ever getting on the back of a motorbike," Holland was saying.

One morning outside the Commercial Hotel, Ellen laughed – a sound no one in town had heard before. A tall waterfall from Africa or the Andes could have been transposed onto their dusty old street.

Apparently her father had said something dry. Looking across at him as he trudged Ellen laughed, and when he gave his two-stage smile, known elsewhere as a *muddy smile*, she tilted her throat and laughed all the more.

A daughter openly mocking a father: other women saw the power of her adult beauty overflowing as gaiety.

Everybody was proud of her; to think that such a beauty in all its rarity was living in their parts.

Conventionally strong men lost their tongues. At the sight of her, some were inflicted with a sort of paralysis. All they could do when Ellen came into town was stand about grinning and gaping. To get around this the lads speeding past the property made it a practice to sound their horns, and filtered by the river and the trunks of hundreds of euca-lypts it reached the house like the faint bellowing of sexually mournful steers.

Of course there were some who boldly marched up and spoke to her. First they had to get past her father. And he was more like a tennis coach than a father, never letting his girl out of his sight. If a gangly young man appeared to bump into them and opened his mouth to say something, or if Holland came out onto the street to find his daughter in the sunlight half-listening to a man, or several of them, he stood beside her with an expression of concentrated shrewdness. Among them he was the expert. After all, she was his daughter; he knew her better than anyone.

The trouble was he was not impressed with any of them. There was something wrong with each and every one, if not in the way they spoke, in the way they looked; one of them held his smile too wide, with another it was the size of thumbs. By far the worst were those who exhibited a certain truculent ease. They literally bulged with familiarity, their hair combed like paddocks for sowing.

They were just beginning, like the country itself; Holland didn't know what to say to them.

His daughter, she had no idea what men took and discarded, how they went about it. Without thinking, Holland had hired a man from town to help grub out some trees, a contentedly married man, known to be reliable – until Holland caught him leaning on his shovel, doing nothing but watching Ellen. Later, he saw him offering her a cigarette. Holland felt as if he himself was being violated. She had always been at his side, had grown alongside him – an extension of himself.

Cars and trucks slowed down approaching the gate; for you never know your luck. Suitors came from all directions. If one knocked on the front door asking for his daughter, Holland was factually polite. One of them galloped up no hands on a horse! Noticing her curious smile Holland pointed out the idiot had been drinking.

In winter she liked to spend entire mornings in the tower where it was warm and she could feed the birds. From there the scale of her father's achievement could be seen;

though when she took off her clothes and felt like an orchid, the all-over warmth opening the petals of her body, she became conscious of her nakedness mocking the laborious placement into all corners of the different species of trees. Other times she sat in her blue room brushing her lovely hair, which reminded Holland of her mother. She made her own clothes. She did sewing and general tidying and could be heard humming in the kitchen. The same small books were read over again. For all her beauty she ate noisily.

In gentle replay of when he had first arrived in the district, invitations were received from the same big houses, and in these houses the tables, the walls, the English clocks and their chimes, the pattern of plates, the side of lamb and boiled potatoes had remained the same. The hesitant young women in florals from Holland's day were larger, looser figures, mothers now with altogether different concerns. And attention this time was directed not really at Holland but his daughter who sat with a straight back, alongside (for instance) a broad-shouldered son clearing his throat in a new shirt. Ellen assumed a distant expression, as if she was obeying the obligations of her father.

Afterwards the man of the house, knowing Holland's interest, would sometimes toss the keys to the son to drive everybody around the property, while Holland sat in the back and identified each eucalypt in the headlights.

"She's a gem, that one of yours," the grazier would concede, meaning Holland's daughter.

Loudly, as well as quietly or through emissaries, it was pointed out a marriage would deliver impressive agricultural synergies, guaranteed to leave a smile on the face of everybody at the table. Holland gave the impression of weighing up each proposition in his hands. With these men he'd look thoughtful and make sucking sounds with his teeth while nodding or offering another cigarette, which is the way they themselves would have handled it, visually.

A certain restlessness entered Ellen's beauty.

The town women and women in the surrounding homesteads looked on and waited. One of the things Holland had learned from his many years observing trees was *don't rush, there is natural speed*. And Ellen, she seemed more comfortable with the careless faces of seasonal workers, the filthy motor mechanics, and the afternoon drinkers; at least with them she looked on, bemused.

Holland said to his daughter, "I want you to promise me something: keep away from the commercial travellers. You've seen them in town with their Windsor knots and their fancy cigarette-lighters. A few have come to the door here, as you well know, thinking we'd buy ribbons and strips of cloth. They carry samples of jewellery and medicines in special suitcases. That little bloke who's been here – moustache – he sells hair oils, soaps and whatnot. I'm told what they do now is spread out a printed catalogue, where you put your finger on something that takes your fancy, and it gets delivered later. I'd say that was very clever."

These were older men who had built dusty careers out of hearing the sounds of their own voices. They worked on commission. They knew when to advance, when to draw back. Holland had seen how the sturdy town women became lovely and childlike under their words. Could they spin a story! As an example, Holland pointed to the coloured curtains he himself had bought from one of these persistent silver-tongues, which had faded after one summer. Yet these natty men had an easy generosity. Later, that same peddler of shonky curtains who specialised in puns and perpetual dirty jokes had volunteered to pick up from a faraway town and deliver to Holland a scarce sample of Silver Princess, of the vaguely musical name, *E. symphyomyrtus*, which Holland then managed after much difficulty to breed in a gully.

"Beware," Holland told his daughter, "beware of any man who deliberately tells a story. You're going to come across men like that. Know what I'm saying?" He wanted to take her hands until they hurt. "I want you to listen to me. There's no real reason for you to be going into town. But leaving that aside: it's worth asking, when a man starts concocting a story in front of you. Why is he telling it? What does he want?"

The idea that Holland's daughter was like the princess locked in the tower of a damp castle was of course false. After all, she was living on a property in western New South Wales. There was plenty of space to move about in. Yet it did seem she had been removed from view – unless she had decided herself to step back. Even if this was partly true – imaginations had taken off running – the slightest suggestion of trapped beauty produces a deeper resonance than plain beauty. It could only add to her desirability; and was Holland's blind spot.

Fellow arborists, politicians, soil-erosion specialists, farmers' delegations, even the occasional tourist who had once been welcomed, were now discouraged. Holland could no longer be sure whether their interest was in the trees or his daughter. A friendly neighbour and son arriving unannounced as they do in the country districts would be received politely; that was about all. If the lanky son was lucky he'd glimpse Ellen's face at a window, as if under water.

Sometimes Ellen was seen across the river among the trees, sliced into verticals: that is, fragments of coloured cloth. Whenever she did step out in her dainty shoes and appear on the main street her beauty was startling – flesh, contoured and speckled.

Holland was conscious of people waiting for him. Each day he woke to a sparkling morning, knowing his trees were arranged outside in their remarkable variety, only to find his daughter-question in all its imprecision still there before him. He was being forced to think about something he hadn't wanted to think about; he wanted to return to thinking about the usual other things. The subject, or rather the situation, wouldn't go away.

The butcher's wife wasn't much help. It became awkward having his cup of tea with her, now joined by her friend next door, the rhythmically nodding postmistress.

"Let the poor girl make up her own mind. How old is she? She knows more about these things than you do. What do you know? A few facts and figures about gum trees. And what use are all your trees now, tell me that? You'll just have to close your eyes with Ellen and hope for the best."

Time and landscape were forever porous; prescribing a

narrow radius for a daughter over undulating ground could never last, not exactly.

Holland decided to take Ellen to Sydney; she was nineteen.

In the big city he imagined she would blend in amongst the criss-crossing movements, the congested numbers.

In fact, everything about her was even more noticeable in Sydney, her beauty given greater contrast by the healthy downright ordinariness of the crowd-majority. As well, he soon realised there was a greater concentration of men; so many formidable men with experienced manners; he was constantly noticing a man or groups of city men running their eyes over his daughter, who appeared completely oblivious.

They stayed in Bondi. Ellen's idea was to go to the beach every day. She wanted to be alone. To his surprise she moved about with ease in other parts of the city, as if the dream-like distances that existed between things on their property meant nothing to her. She got him to buy her a pair of fancy sunglasses. He had always bought all Ellen's clothes, including underclothes. There was always something he felt she should be wearing. When she raced out in the morning and returned in the evening she appeared, to her father, tall and shining.

Although he said very little he was irritable. When he sat in the foyer or out on the footpath his nose felt too big. There was nothing much to do. He kept looking at his hands. A golden age when men stained their fingers tribally with nicotine. What these red-brown hands had produced – eucalypts, demonstrating diversity – did not seem necessary in the city. And so on and on he fretted; waiting for his daughter. This happened to be their last trip together.

He had always been a poor sleeper. She remembered as a child he had told her about special ways of getting to sleep, ways which relied entirely on a numbing visual sameness, which he exaggerated while he was shaving, to make her laugh. Now the light showed under his door, and she could hear her father creaking about at all hours.

Finally, he emerged from the office and entered her bedroom.

They spoke for some time; Ellen wept.

The same day Holland's decision became known. It was simple enough. The man who correctly named every eucalypt on the property would win the hand of his daughter, Ellen.

At first there was a kind of milky silence; people couldn't believe their ears. By the time it appeared as a story in the papers, young hopefuls and others not so young were already preparing themselves.

5

Marginata

A BRIEF WORD about the town; we'll keep it short, in homage to the main street.

It was small and yellowish. Anywhere else it would be called a "village". It could even be a "hamlet": there was no church.

Otherwise it was a town that had *only one of everything*: hotel, bank, post office, picture theatre, a few shops displaying buckets, bolts of cloth, agricultural products and canvas awnings reaching down to the gutters in summer. It had one blonde, one man with one arm (El Alamein), one thief, one woman who could have been a witch. There was one person who wanted to be liked by everyone, one who always had the last word, one who felt trapped by marriage.

Tibooburra, further west, is known for the pile of hot boulders at the end of its one and only main street. Other towns achieve distinction with unavoidable monuments, such as merino rams or pineapples forty times their normal height, or the hand-lettered boast on the outskirts that this town has recorded the hottest temperature in Australia, or is the tidiest in the state – therefore, to be avoided; Mossman, in northern Queensland, has a sugar train most days hissing and pissing along its main street. This one – the yellowish town – has a dogleg throwing out the line of the street, so unexpected and yet in harmony with the outstretched verandahs it endowed the otherwise ordinary town with mass-reproduction qualities.

Most of Ellen's suitors lived in the town or the nearby countryside, and the town became a staging post for the second wave, quietly determined optimists from other parts, including distant cities, the way Zanzibar in the last century was used by perspiring, single-minded British explorers setting forth into the interior.

The town filtered the suitors. Some didn't get beyond the hotel. Men made their way to the town out of sexual curiosity, casual plunderers who fancied their chances: after all, they could spot at a glance a Blue Gum, a Yellow Box, even the stunted *calycogona*, and quote its ridiculous nickname, Gooseberry Mallee. But they received a shock when actually confronted with the bewildering fact of so many eucalypts in the one spot, so many obscure species, and the stories of early failure of those who had gone before them, including well-qualified timber-cutters and the despondent local schoolteacher.

After a while these men drifted away without even seeing the speckled prize. One chap in a wool suit stepped off the train from Yass, made his way out to Holland's property, patting all the dogs on the way, took one look at the expanse of trees from the gate, turned around and went straight back home. More calculating ones who had not underestimated the test began by swotting up on the vast subject, their noses in inadequate botanical books.

Take Jarrah (*E. marginata*). Is there anyone not *baffled* by Jarrah – its hardness, its degree of difficulty? There is civil disobedience in its nature. Still, it should be admitted material difficulties can deepen the beauty of timber. The impulse is always to pick up and admire a piece of Jarrah – stroke it like a cat. Is it possible to say a piece of timber is "proud"? Unlike those that split at the slightest blow: that is, the skinny shivering pine, the spineless acacia? Jarrah had quite a name for endurance under the ground and under water. Streets were paved with it in Mediterranean Sydney and Marvellous Melbourne, the wood long outlasting the men who cut it into lengths, not to mention the loyal floorboards in ballrooms and grand hotels.

Handsome tree, straight and tall, it won't cultivate in plantations. (Cussedness, again.) Holland once had a stepfather called Jarraby, known to be proud, stubborn.

Away from Western Australia few people would know a Jarrah tree, even if they bumped into one.

Now it happened that the local schoolteacher was the early favourite to win Ellen's hand because he possessed the double qualification of an education and a real affinity for wood; carving heavy bowls for sensitive fruits such as peaches and grapes had become his solitary pastime. Sure enough, by lunchtime on the first day he had correctly named eighty-seven eucalypts, and was doing it well when he went blank at the fatly handsome Jarrah up against the fence behind the house.

"Take your time," Holland said, and cleared his throat. "No use going like a rat up a drainpipe," he wanted to say.

He liked the young teacher. And there was no need to

rush. As always it is fatal to panic. From the densities of Sydney the young teacher had been transferred to the country, a difficult lesson in drabness. Several times he had seen Ellen on the main street. Late afternoons and Sundays he walked along the dirt road, past the Salmon Gum, hoping she might emerge. And the property itself, all those broad acres of river frontage, big old homestead, barely came into the teacher's equation at all.

On the point of saying "Jarrah!" one eye became entangled in the foliage of the Karri (*E. diversicolor*) nearby.

"That's too bad," Holland stubbed his cigarette. "That's a shame. I had you down as a real chance."

Before setting out, each suitor was invited into the house – into the parlour, no less – for a cup of tea. Holland could sit back and examine them. In a real sense the test began there and then. Coming forward to serve them was the prize herself, more speckled, certainly more beautiful than they remembered or had ever imagined, allowing a glimpse of cleavage and a shadow of what appeared to be faint consternation.

From the day her father made his decision on the marriage question she hardly knew what to say to him, or anyone. No ancient grandmother, wise mother or interested sisters were at hand to help. It hardly mattered that the eucalyptus test would sort out the contestants, wheat from the chaff and all that, a process simultaneously healthy and unhealthy, as her father put it. "Only a man with golden hair, a golden-haired boy out of the ordinary, is going to name all these trees – someone like your old father here," he had said to her.

The early suitors were all locals. At the sight of some she couldn't help laughing, until her father said, "That'll do now!"

One was a retired shearer, old enough to be her grandfather – no teeth. The town's one and only part-time plumber put on a virtuoso display of relaxation on the floral sofa, stretching out his legs and calling for another cup of tea, only to step out the front door and fail to identify the very first tree he pointed to, the Black Peppermint, which is as common as rain. Even Holland gave a small laugh. Many who managed to reach eighty or more without a stumble were knocked out by a common roadside gum; lack of concentration, according to Holland. Another one who knew timber but not trees was young Kevin who had lost his arm working for a sawmill. Surprising how many failed to spot the single Ironbark intruder in the windbreak.

Needless to say there were men who tried to bluff, or laugh their way through, or devise delaying tactics. Such ruses which can be seen as extensions of character had served them in the past. The sore loser became angry when he lost! Others offered money. Why not? It was the full world on display, in miniature. One or two tried to enter via the side door, as it were: "Isn't there some other way we could arrange this? Can't we sit down and discuss it? What I know about gum trees would fit on the head of a pin, but I do know I'd be a good man for your daughter." The bank manager sent his short-sighted son. A dark stranger from another town claimed a photographic memory: accordingly, the first eucalypt he had never seen before finished him. Silence was generally ingrained; only a few never stopped talking. Now and then Ellen in her room could hear a loud voice from a sloping paddock. Performers from a passing circus had heard the story of the beautiful daughter and argued for too long about drawing lots. One of the nattiest of the dangerous commercial travellers put his name forward; Holland went into town and talked him out of it.

Evidently the very idea of a test to win a man's daughter was either nerve-racking or else altogether too strange: suitors were known to have drunk seven schooners an hour before. A country jockey fronted up accompanied by his strapper who mentioned to Ellen the jockey was already married. "I'll have to take a squiz at a leaf," said another one. "For that I'll need a ladder." At the sight of these men dolled up for the occasion in a new shirt and haircut Ellen felt a faint shift into sadness, the flutter of a white bird in a cage; others came as they were; some stank. A procession; all sizes.

Ellen didn't really like the look of any of them.

These were men willing to bypass the traditional words, whispers and hesitancies, the cajoling and the hopeful jokes and the clumsy shoulder-stroking, the incredible attentiveness which will sap a man's energy, deliberate absentmindedness as well, which form a mosaic of *necessary slowness* . . . It allows the woman to choose the man, while giving the man the illusion it is he who has taken her. Whereas – outside the yellowish town – these suitors who had arrived to line up for the test could, in a sense, reach the same goal with their backs turned, reciting facts. It wasn't even necessary to look in her direction (the schoolteacher was the exception – his downfall).

"Yessiree, these country types," Holland complained, "they give the impression they know the land inside out, but ask them and they can't tell you the names of ordinary things in front of them. We can be talking here about a eucalypt that's as common as the flies."

It began to occur to Ellen that the degree of difficulty was so extreme only a few men on earth could name all the eucalypts; aside from her father, that is, in his dark coat. This might go on for years, with no result. And she began to relax, prematurely.

The trouble was the degree of difficulty activated one of the laws of curiosity: as each man who stepped forward failed, and the flood of suitors reduced to a trickle, the unattainability of the prize increased Ellen's desirability still further.

Holland and his daughter were apparently oblivious to this. Now that the matrimonial question was more or less settled their visits to town resumed, where Ellen was immediately looked at and discussed with fresh calculation.

It was summer. The trunks of trees were hot. In the river, where smooth stones lay under water like pears suspended in syrup, Ellen kicked and floated, and examined her arms as she dangled her legs from the bridge.

Then a New Zealander burst through the air, striding up the drive to present himself. He had an intense moustache. His hair too was as dark as Dunedin. Before each eucalypt he stroked the moustache, and began to annoy Holland by laughing to himself as he struggled to name one of the more obscure species.

"By God, though, he knows his eucalypts," Holland said with respect. "And he doesn't even live here. He's a funny one. I caught him yesterday praying by the gate, just before he was about to start."

By the third day the New Zealander had passed the halfway stage.

It was enough for Holland to chew thoughtfully on his toast, while Ellen could hardly swallow, imagining what it would be like living every day with such a man. And she felt strange knowing word of her plight had reached people in another country. Her father couldn't stop shaking his head at how a man on the South Island had managed to become an expert on eucalypts; a real mystery to him. Eucalypts were native to Australia and nowhere else. He would have been amazed if more than fifty different eucalypts had been transplanted in the whole of New Zealand. On the morning of the fourth day Holland was on the point of asking a few questions when the man came up against, and was defeated by, one of the many Stringybarks, a scraggy-looking *E. youmanii*, which could easily fool a professional botanist, and he left with a relieved nod, for the first time looking into Ellen's face.

The story of Holland and his beautiful daughter had crossed the Tasman; it travelled too up the centre of Australia, along the Stuart Highway, filling up with petrol on the way. It spread out from the highway, left and right, like the trunk and branches on a tree. As a consequence, a *smiling Chinaman* knocked on the door, all the way from Darwin. To Holland he gave a slight bow and said he was a merchant of fruit and vegetables.

Everything he touched made him happy. He had what are called "eyes as sweet as sugar". When Ellen poured him tea he smiled, "Nice hand you have." Ellen decided he would live to a great age. (A vague feeling, rather than a physiological fact: that an energetic brain can drag the body along for a few extra yards. Long are the lives of the philosophers.)

At the same time, Ellen wondered if this happy man had experienced envy or jealousy, the confusions of loneliness – the usual mess – not to mention anything more serious, such as sudden gusts of despair.

There he was now under the guise of oriental cheerfulness sifting through his taxonomy of botanical names and fitting them to a general appearance of a tree. Naturally he was stronger on the subtropical species from the Darwin area. Taking things more cautiously than the Kiwi, now and then standing back to say, "Ahhhh . . . " at an especially graceful specimen, such as the Flooded Gum which formed an accidental triangle with the Silver Gimlet and the double-trunked Red Mallee (*E. socialis*), and constantly blowing on a red handkerchief for good luck, he hardly faltered, but smiled a little longer at difficult-to-recognise foliage.

Nine days later he was still smiling. And his mouth began to remind Holland of his own father.

"Who'd want someone grinning like that around the house all day?" he said to Ellen. "Don't worry, he's going to come a gutser, I can feel it. I don't know how he's got this far. How old would you say he was? I can't make him out."

It finally took a eucalypt from the southern tip of Tasmania that doesn't look like a eucalypt at all.

The Chinaman actually tripped over it.

The Varnished Gum (*E. vernicosa*) is more like a shrub or a creeper. It barely comes up to a man's knees. Buds and fruits are in threes; the varnished leaves.

The suitors were reduced to those with a professional knowledge of the subject. The idea of winning the hand of a man's daughter by naming all his trees, and the chances of any one man succeeding, were discussed in staff-rooms throughout the country. When a year passed, then almost another, and with still no winner, the difficulty of the test itself rather than the prize became more and more the attraction. These specialists in botany and forestry were like those great champions in the Olympics who preserve their strength and exert psychological pressure on their rivals by waiting until the bar has been raised to an extreme height before even bothering to compete.

Ellen watched as her father in his shabby coat greeted them. Aside from tree-worshippers and the red-haired tree-surgeon from Brisbane there were the watertable specialists, national-tree zealots, the eucalyptus oil patent-penders, and a world authority on barks who had visited the property before, leading a delegation.

"You wouldn't want one of them," her father conceded. "All the experts I know have their heads in the sand, one way or another. They've worked themselves into a corner. And look at you! You're a princess, too good for most men, at least the ones I've come across. There's got to be one somewhere who fits the bill. Nobody's perfect, I know that. But you seem to have lost interest. What's your opinion? This is taking up a lot more time than I thought. Is there anyone you've met who's caught your eye, even for a split second? I can see I'm going to go to the grave without being any the wiser."

Ellen had gone pleasantly distant. One arm went gradually cold.

Really, what sort of man could go and name all the trees? Her father, of course; he, though, was different. The sheer number of names shifting about in English and Latin would occupy vital space in a person, space that could be used for other, more natural things, the way an unsuccessful dealer in farm machinery allows the accumulation of rusty trade-ins to encroach on the front, side and backyards of his weatherboard house.

"Our man is going to come from one of the cities," her father predicted. "That's my gut feeling."

Listening to her father and more or less daydreaming Ellen was unable to picture such an all-knowing person, let alone whether anything about him would interest her. And isolated in the bluestone homestead, surrounded by the trees in question, she felt anyway the answer all seemed far away. The problem was always over the next hill. It encouraged the casual, fatalistic manner.

Holland received a letter.

"Hello, it says here Mister Roy Cave is throwing his hat into the ring. He's got his secretary to type it. I've heard about him. He's got quite a name in the eucalyptus world.

He's from Adelaide," he told Ellen. "People used to joke he had personally inspected every single eucalypt in the state of South Australia. Adelaide, the city of eucalypts. So they say. He grew up with the gum trees. Are you listening? Says here he's taking his annual holidays. Would it be convenient, etc.? He's booked into the pub. He means business! We're going to have him breathing down our necks for weeks."

The father moved to the window and with hands clasped behind his back adopted a father's pose of gazing over his park-like property, which represented his daughter's prospects. It included delicate curves, pale brown grasses, liquid flow and heat.

"Are you getting tired of this?" he suddenly turned. "God knows what's going to happen. With your mother and me the unexpected took over completely. It was an awkward business at the time, the whole thing was very awkward. On the bright side we came through; I'm still here; and with you."

6

Maculata

THE BEAUTY OF this tree ... lies in the smooth, clean-looking bark. This is shed in irregular patches, leaving small dimples – hence Spotted Gum – and as the bark surface ages it changes colour from cream to blue-grey, pink or red, giving a mottled appearance. The trunk is generally erect and symmetrical.

The flowers are borne in rather large, compound inflorescences, whilst the fruits are ovoid, with short necks and deeply enclosed valves.

And so on and so forth.

The juvenile leaves may be a foot long with the petiole entering above the base. The adult leaves are lanceolate, falcate, almost equally green on both sides.

In conversation Mr Cave employed with lip-smacking relish the terms "petiole", "inflorescences", "falcate" and "lanceolate", and he was also comfortable with "sessile", "fusiform" and "conculorous". Holland who had never bothered with the technicalities sometimes wondered what on earth Mr Cave was talking about.

Spotted Gums occur mainly on rather heavy soils, especially clay loams derived from shales, where the species is often associated with Grey Box (*E. moluccana*) and ironbarks.

The species was first described in 1844 by J. D. Hooker, the botanist on the exploration ship *Erebus*. His early writings were on the flora of Tasmania. Hooker, one of those fact-embracing Victorians, prodigious in his appetite for classification and verification – a friend and supporter of Darwin. There was so much to do, so much to record. He could scarcely sit still for his studio photograph: the mutton-chop whiskers, hand of the worn-out wife resting on his shoulder. He was afraid of dying too soon. For Hooker, the naming and classifying of things lay at the heart of understanding the world; at least it offered that illusion. He died at ninety-four. Another example – entirely at random – of a hyperactive mind signalling the body along? Where did he, as they say, find the time? Joseph Hooker's *The Flora of British India* alone is seven volumes.

He succeeded his father as Director of Kew Gardens, London. And like his father before him his own name was given a descriptive prefix, denoting a higher classification: Joseph Dalton Hooker was made a Sir; for services to trees.

Mr Cave had visited Kew some time before he arrived at Holland's. It goes without saying that he made a beeline for the eucalypts, ignoring the representative trees and shrubs and ferns from every country under the sun ("the oaks are thought to be holy trees in Lithuania"), the way a man in a great museum hurries past the rows of patiently begging masterpieces just to see one particular oil in an obscure corner – a tunnel vision virtually impossible to practise in a zoo.

Mr Cave had assumed like any reasonable person that among the many eucalypts at Kew there would be a Spotted Gum planted in homage to their man who first described it. He also assumed it would be in a prominent position. But, no: of the two *and only two* eucalypts he managed to find after numerous directions one was a struggling Snow Gum (*E. pauciflora*), verging on the dispirited, and the other, outside the ladies' lavatories with the louvres, a Cider Gum (*E. gunnii*). True, *E. gunnii* was also first described by Joseph Hooker; but the Spotted Gum is more beautiful than the Cider Gum. Connoisseurs claim it is the most eye-catching eucalypt of them all.

Mr Cave checked the identifying label for accuracy, and although he didn't want to be seen loitering around the lavatories paced about in front of the tree.

The eucalypt looked out of place, perfunctory, ignored. A vagina-like slit had opened up in the lower trunk, as if in patriotic protest at its transportation and isolation. Women kept coming and going. Some were pretty, with children. Mr Cave kept pacing and standing back from the gum tree, unable to leave.

At this point in the story he sat down on a bench and twiddled his thumbs. He didn't know what else to do in England. Anyone seeing him would think he was being rueful.

Vagueness was not something he normally felt; vaguely then he became conscious of a woman near the tree. She'd been glancing this way and that in a strange manner. She was slightly plump and wore a scarf over her head. Then leaving her child in its pram she hurried back and in the one movement dropped an envelope into the slit of the tree.

At least that's what he thought he saw. On the bench he'd been thinking his years were measured in strokes of trees, and some were angled, a few stunted. The intervals were rhythmic, almost musical. His history was stuffed with trees. Now he was staring at the solitary *E. gunnii* which by rights should have been a *maculata*.

He was half-deciding whether to get up and take another look or merely wander away, for it was time, when a young gardener appeared. He lowered his wheelbarrow and in full view thrust his arm up to his elbow into the vagina-slit of the Cider Gum – something he wouldn't want to try in Australia. Mr Cave watched as he opened the envelope. Shoving it in his back pocket he immediately took it out again. With a sigh he looked around smiling, when he noticed Cave.

The private scene in two parts Mr Cave had witnessed would stay with him for the rest of his life. It was perhaps prompted by the surrounding green, brighter than any lawn. The shadows formed spikes and lattice. They were unusually dark. And the necessary eagerness, first of the woman, which then activated the eagerness of the younger gardener. The man's muddy boots. The interval between their actions; the difference in their years. Pink patterned scarf.

And, for all that, not knowing what was written on the

note, who they were; the open-endedness of it all, like the late afternoon itself.

Not long after that Mr Cave decided in his deliberate way he would win the hand of Holland's speckled daughter.

7

Regnans

"TALL TIMBER" – a term used locally by the Sprunt sisters in unison to render male flesh abstract. Seated on the sofa reserved for suitors, Mr Cave protruded from a bed of blushing roses, shoulders almost coming up to Ellen's. It is hard to imagine a more unsuitable name than Cave for someone so straight and tall. Accordingly, people forgot about his first name, Roy, and tacked on Mister in front. "Cave" implies the horizontal, whereas this man was vertical – a telegraph pole fashioned from a tree.

What interested Ellen was his hair. At first she thought it was as black as a crow. Then she remembered the pair of shoes she'd liked in Sydney, small and glossy blue-black, parted like Mr Cave's hair to one side, which is why she looked upon him favourably.

He was almost old enough to be Ellen's father; yet where her father's face had become a reddish terrain of boulders, ravines, flood plains and spinifex, Mr Cave's face was magically smooth. It didn't generate any lines, not even when he talked. The black hair can be set in context: appar- ently it was part and parcel, a healthy by-product, of self-possession. The only lines on his person came from the crisp safari suit, a khaki construct of paramilitary lines, like a jacket sketched in pencil, pointing up to his face where, except for his carefully combed parting, there were no lines.

Those vertical lines from the unfortunate safari suit helped make him appear taller than he actually was.

Talking to Mr Cave, Holland nodded more than usual; at the same time he offered a grain of patience – unusual for him – which grew into a canny watchfulness. It wasn't that Holland was showing respect; hardly. In the world of eucalypts everyone knew about Mr Cave, but then they knew all about Holland and his trees too.

In Mr Cave's Adelaide, the distinction between city and country, as proposed by the Greeks, was blurred. The country penetrates the city almost to the town hall steps, depositing gum trees on the way, along with vast rectangles of dry grass. As a consequence, Adelaide people may be said to possess a certain physical clarity of country people, at the same time a blurriness within and careful faces from crossing daily the boundaries between city and country, and back again.

Meanwhile, Ellen wanted to reach out and touch the blackness of Mr Cave's hair. So much so she had to hold back a laugh.

"How are your teeth?" her father shouted. "Try one of my daughter's rock cakes!"

Food as a therapeutic offering between strangers has never been satisfactorily explained. Here is an ordinary-looking action which goes far deeper than mere hospitality. By producing food and presenting in full view a portion to a stranger, a woman is offering an extension of herself; it can be enjoyed, but is not flesh. All he, the stranger, is allowed is a morsel representing the woman. A fragment is all. She remains the giver, but at one remove.

This use of food as a medium – giving while denying – and without a bitter aftertaste – has harsh origins, rather obviously among the nomads. Food as an interceptor, as a *deflector*! It may be said to continue to this day as a protection in married life.

And Mr Cave was now demonstrating the deeply held process by accepting one of Ellen's slightly burnt rock cakes matter-of-factly, not quite acknowledging her, like the peevish date-eaters of *Arabia deserta*. Then removing any crumbs from his creases and pleats he placed them one by one on his tongue.

"I'm nothing more than an amateur," Holland reminded their visitor. "And an amateurish one at that."

They were talking about others in their field.

"Did you ever come across . . . " Mr Cave began click-clicking his ballpoint – the frustration. "His name was, what's his name? It was the name of an English town."

Ellen smiled. She liked him for saying that.

Straining to remember the surname of the man whose speciality was said to be the Northern Territory species her father screwed his face up like a dog while, equally deter-mined, their black-haired visitor sat still, his face smooth in concentration more like an elbow.

"You don't mean Hungerford?"

"No, he's in grapes. And this one passed away. A tractor rolled over him. You must have exchanged letters during your researches."

"I haven't kept up with the experts for years," said Holland. "Once I got this place up and running I didn't need any experts." Holland gave a laugh. "These days they're more inclined to make contact with me, I'm now the receiver of letters. I've had them writing to me from overseas as if I have all the answers."

It was after ten-thirty and Mr Cave hadn't made a move. He showed no sign of nerves. On the verandah he stretched his long legs out on one of the planters' chairs. Without yet bothering to identify a single tree he already was making it look easy.

Ellen couldn't remember the last time her father had talked to anyone on the verandah for more than three minutes, aside from herself. "I'm the encyclopaedia around here!" he once said in a kind of triumphant good humour. Her father was a man who didn't have any close friends, she noticed. Yet there he was leaning against the verandah post, a reminder to Ellen that she would always associate cigarette smoke with him and the texture of his clothing.

Mr Cave was smoking too.

"Eucalypts dominate the streetscapes of Adelaide, more than any other city. The things are everywhere." (A sure sign of confidence: to call eucalypts "things".) "We had a *fasciculosa* and a *cosmophylla* growing in the backyard, the next-door neighbours had the finest Candlebark Gum you'd ever be likely to see, and there was a quite outstanding *megacarpa* on the footpath. You see what I'm saying? At school we were taught to recognise different timbers by their grain, and we'd be hit and hit hard with a polished wooden ruler if we missed one. I had the methodical mind

77

drummed into me. At school, to fill in time, did you chuck gumnuts at each other? There were eucalypts in the school yard; *cladocalyx*, if I'm not mistaken. We had eucalypts coming out of our ears."

"I don't know exactly what happened to me," Holland said more or less in reply. "I came here and I planted one, then I planted another. Other parts of the property needed a tree. I kept going. At a certain point I had passed a threshold; I couldn't go back or leave the plantings as they were. By then the whole situation became . . . what do you say? An end in itself. Everything about eucalypts was interesting. Before the trees I didn't have a clue about anything much. The eucalypts gave me an interest."

"They grow on you," Mr Cave went extra-passive at his joke. "Something else happened to me, I think this had a bearing." He looked out over the trees. "My mother had subscription tickets to the Adelaide Symphony Orchestra. Always the same two seats. Remember the way regulars used to have their names stencilled on church pews? And always sitting in front of us was a Miss Dora Heron, a woman in mauve, who never opened her mouth. To keep everybody's germs at bay she kept dabbing eucalyptus oil onto her hanky from a little jar throughout the concert, whatever was playing. Those seated around her, myself, my mother, couldn't escape the fumes. On top of everything else, no wonder eucalypts took a deep grip on me." Mr Cave shifted in his seat. "Mind you, it's given me a life of sorts." He began nodding. "Everything is a comparison," he said for no apparent reason.

Ellen had been standing by the window. It was odd how

two men repeatedly put down blocks of matter and left it at that. In tone and steadiness they were tarpaulined trucks with heavy loads, now and then changing down a gear, rather than light and sprightly birds, hopping from one bit of colour to another.

Mr Cave stood up. "Let's look at a few of these things of yours," he said with ominous casualness.

And Holland let go of the bevelled verandah post as Mr Cave made his way over to the Black Peppermint which had snookered the town's part-time plumber, so commonplace to Roy Cave he hardly gave it a glance, then on to the Blue Gum which can be seen on the dry hills of Algeria, South Africa and California, and the Silvertop Stringybark by the gate which opened the long narrow paddock alongside the house, sloping up to the treeline. There, eucalypts were dotted about in apparent randomness, in every direction.

To Ellen, Mr Cave appeared to be strolling ahead with her father in tow – an optical illusion which increased over distance. So tall was the suitor that her father looked like an old jumps-jockey hurrying after the owner or trainer for instructions. In fact, Holland was giving the instructions as he ticked off each tree identified.

If a species presented any difficulty Mr Cave said, "What is it we have *here*?"

Otherwise, he sauntered, one paddock at a time, one tree followed by the next, methodical, very methodical. It was altogether shocking in its steadiness; he was always going forward. Continuing the display of relaxation he often paused between trees to talk about something entirely different.

By one-thirty he decided he was finished for the day.

*   *

Tall trees breed even taller stories. There was once a woman
called Thistle. If a man touched her on any part his skin
turned blue, a permanent blue, so people would see he had
touched Thistle. One day Ellen would be told about a man
in Scotland (Highlands?) who would never talk to anyone
under six feet tall. Her father, not so long ago, had read
out a story in the morning newspaper about a sixty-three-
year-old woman in Brazil who had been X-rayed after
complaining of stomach pains and was found to be carrying
the skeleton of a foetus conceived outside her womb up to
fifteen years earlier. Imagine a man on a property in western
New South Wales setting out single-handedly to plant every
known eucalypt, the property and the man's life trans-
formed to that purpose. Ellen one day overheard the
postmistress, "She made a necklace out of lavatory chains.
She was very clever." A man drowned himself in the River
Murray at Mildura by weighing himself down with German
dictionaries and German encyclopaedias. Another man, just
retired, and not so long ago, swam the entire length of the
Murray – from its source to its mouth – suffering severe
cramps and getting snagged and sunburnt in the process,
pleased in the end to have done something no one else
had done, let alone (his words) "even dreamed of". All the
people in one small town – it would have to be Eastern
Europe – were deaf, except one. What happened then
was – "According to my mother," Ellen was told by the
small woman in town, "I was conceived under a gum tree."
She had eyes set close to her nose like glove buttons. In
Iceland a young man leaving home for America spent the

night before his departure counting all the wrinkles on his grandmother's face. Do you believe in ghosts? There was the story of the brave woman who put on secret trousers and became a "man" for an hour. Stories of everlasting depth are told at night. What about the lady who saved the town of Coventry by riding through the streets naked on a white horse? It has to be a story because the horse is white. Man falls in love with a *river*. Young man in perfect health spends a night with a woman and leaves a tooth behind.

The tallest trees have the tiniest seeds. "Great oaks from little acorns grow." Obviously the Europeans who produced that maxim could not have seen the larger eucalypts. A monarch such as *E. regnans*, which shakes the earth when it falls and provides enough timber to build a three-bedroom house, grows from a seed scarcely larger than the following full stop.

In the days when timber-workers in Victoria and Tasmania were photographed measuring the girth of gigantic trees it was subsequently announced – it was repeatedly trumpeted abroad, the way a film star's vital statistics were once made public – that *Eucalyptus regnans*, better known as Mountain Ash, was the tallest tree in the world, just as Salzburg is said to have the highest suicide rate in the world, surpassing anything the United States had to offer. After the most rigorous measurements possible were taken in the congested forests at least two Mountain Ash were found to be over 100 metres high; one reportedly came in at 140 metres.

Naturally in the rural parts of Australia it was a matter of quiet satisfaction that something native was the world's best, or at least could not be beaten when it came to size. The anxieties of youth are displayed in the New World; phallic symbols, as they were once called, are seized upon, along with military defeats, to brandish in triumph.

For their part the Americans could not accept the verdict. As far as America was concerned the sequoia of California reigned over the world of trees. They didn't have to wait long for the position to be restored. In less than a generation the tallest *E. regnans* began losing their tops in storms or lightning strikes! Either that or one or two of the surveyors' original measurements were faulty. What is the reason – the underlying impulse – for exaggeration? It is most noticeable immediately before and after a person's death.

8

Signata

THERE ARE FIVE different Scribbly Gums, like five brothers in mythology, each bearing a significant name: *sclerophylla, signata, rossii, racemosa* and – see the red rim of its fruit – *haemastoma*.

The Scribbly Gum is concentrated in and around Sydney; only *E. signata*, for example, is found along a narrow coastal strip of northern New South Wales and – state boundaries having no meaning to trees and weeds – protrudes into southern Queensland.

Eventually all five had been transplanted on Holland's property, although the smallest, *E. rossii*, grew at an angle in juvenile protest.

The distinctive calligraphic markings on the trunks left by the tunnelling of insect larvae resemble scribbled words, hasty signatures. It is the almost human qualities of these "scribbles", idly composed, invariably elegant, that draw our eye: there may well be a secret message written on this tree.

E. signata here can represent all five Scribbly Gums.

For a long time Ellen found herself staring in wonder whenever her father wrote his signature. It always began with the forefinger vibrating on the one spot, as if he was intent on squashing an insect, before suddenly breaking free with a circular flourish. Once she actually let out a laugh of horror as his pen tore a hole in the ruled writing paper. The signature itself was as knotted and twisted as a cluster of mallees – low-grade eucalypts with shallow roots. When he set about acquiring from all over Australia dozens of selected tubestock, as the seedlings are called, his cheques were often returned for verification.

As the tree-growing programme spread around the property Holland found it necessary to compile an anthography.

The little black book went with him everywhere. He kept it under his pillow like a grubby Gideon. Each page recorded each eucalypt, its location and date of planting, special characteristics, supplier's name. After the butcher misquoted him, Holland was fond of referring to the catalogue as his "cattle-dog"; anything to be light-hearted about it.

It was not an ordinary catalogue. Trudging across paddocks encouraged rumination. Holland jotted down in pencil all kinds of things. Unfortunately just about all of them fall into the category of homilies; *rest is rust*, for example – it doesn't tell us very much.

But on another page he scribbled something altogether more interesting, *nothing is one*. There we have a multiple truth on offer, something to live by, or at least to believe in; an attempt at texture. *Nothing is one* is repeated on several pages, and by repeating it Holland appeared to endorse it, although aside from the multiplication of the eucalypts – his belief in variety – it hardly showed as his life-principle.

All this scribbling on Holland's property multiplied as Ellen reached marriage age.

At that time Ellen wrote many more words than she spoke. In her journal she described conversations with herself, and real and imaginary conversations with her father; there were descriptions of certain large birds, of the sea and the school gates in Sydney; also recorded were unusual dreams, and impressions of many of the visiting suitors, the latest being Mr Cave. The journal had a silver cover decorated with coloured stars. Within its pages she could discuss her feelings. It was her best friend. There she confided, she floated away. It was all softness in its privacy, a fluttering enfolding world. Ellen especially liked the moment she opened a clean page and the sunlight came in a white fold onto the bed. Then she felt curled up, warm and enclosed in her thoughts; and the dry strokes of the eucalypts and the undulating land outside no longer existed.

A few of the eliminated suitors made direct appeals to her. These Ellen read with interest and sympathy even. Some had used a stub of pencil; one, on butcher's paper. Their humorous misspellings! Sometimes she felt sorry for men. A large sheet of paper arrived from one called Thomas Leigh, who Ellen remembered had spent years somewhere in Italy. It was almost incomprehensible; it might well have been in a secret language. It was really a composition of scribbles, adjustments, half-starts, rubbing-outs and space; she was intrigued by its general delicacy though, and in the bottom corner he'd drawn what appeared to be a tree. As for the local schoolteacher, his elimination released a creek

85

flow of gentle notes, eloquent, honest and resigned, as well as a couple of fruit bowls he'd carved out of Karri or Jarrah, just for her.

Until now Ellen believed her father knew all there was to know about a given subject. It was enough to look at the accumulation of years in his face, and his brevity when answering questions of a factual nature – for it too suggested stored-up knowledge. And importantly his voice was always there. Certainly she found it impossible to imagine another man on earth naming all the eucalypts; anyone succeeding would have to be like her father, only more so.

As for the marriage being more or less arranged by her father, her original shock had been hysterical, that was all. She now regarded it with curiosity, little more. Each and every suitor had fallen by the wayside. Only a few had managed to pass the halfway mark.

So far Mr Cave was the most impressive; the way he took his time, hands in pockets, should have been a warning. Instead of following his progress Ellen wondered to herself and in the pages of her journal why he avoided looking in her direction. "Does he like me?" Taking part in the contest may have been nothing more than a sort of intellectual exercise, a way to fill in his annual holidays.

Her father came into the house with a windswept, baffled look.

"He's good, he's more than good. It's because his mother's gone soft in the head. She doesn't remember him. He's been cast adrift. He's got nothing else to live for. That's all I can think of."

And he began nodding, "Mister Roy Cave is an interesting man in more ways than one."

Poor man, a bachelor. Ellen tried imagining the mother.

"Remember me pointing out – many times – that stunted-looking mallee at the back of the dam – the one I thought was finished but came good? Mount Imlay Mallee: it's one of the rarest eucalypts. It took me years to get hold of it, and even longer to get it to grow. Very few people except you and I have ever seen one with their own eyes. So, as we came towards it, I thought, This'll stop him in his tracks, and I'll have to find another good man for my daughter. But no, he reeled off the proper name, *imlayensis*, in the middle of talking about his mother's furniture. I felt like saying, 'Hey, hold your horses!' He wasn't interested in examining the tree closely. I find that pretty strange. By the way, we could see you hanging out the washing. Guess what? Next he tells me – mentions in passing, if you know what I mean – that our Jarrah is a subspecies. It's called *marginata* – I knew that – but goes by the secondary name *thalassica*."

Holland began laughing in admiration.

"All these eucalypts in the one spot – this'd have to be paradise for him."

But whenever the topic turned to eucalypts it went in one ear and out Ellen's other. And – besides – absorbed in her own thoughts and confusions just then she didn't understand what her father was implying.

The realisation that Mr Cave had well and truly passed the halfway mark struck her on the fifth day. From the tower she saw the two figures traversing a distant paddock. One tall, the other at his elbow untidily familiar.

And she saw – realised – the number of paddocks already accounted for, their combined acreage, containing *hundreds of eucalypts*. Even as she looked the man identified another one, then moved on to the next, and another one. This man was steadily advancing, not rushing. Nothing would stop him!

She couldn't think straight.

As she scrambled down the steps and reached the hall she bumped into the walls, and opened and closed doors.

She sat down and stood up.

In her bedroom she sat down again. She didn't know what to do, where to go.

How did this happen? she wanted to know. And why hadn't she seen it before? She kept asking, What can I do? None of the suitors had been taken seriously; as far as her father was concerned, they were all idiots. It would be like him to concoct such a test believing there wasn't a man on earth who could win.

In the bathroom she turned the taps on full blast, something her father never allowed. Already she saw him being friendly, more than friendly, with Mr Cave. It was mutual respect. Apparently they had a lot in common, the trees for one, and now her. And yet Mr Cave was nothing like her father, not at all.

There was no one else. Mr Cave was so sure of himself he took it easy. By two o'clock he was usually back at his hotel. And on the first weekend he was proposing to take a rest.

Ellen began scribbling letters to her father. Most she tore up, or pasted into her journal. Some Ellen *posted*, even when she could hear him moving about in his room. The first addressed to him she propped against his teacup at breakfast, when all the man wanted to do was read the paper.

"What's this then?" Holland tried holding the pages at arm's length. "You used to have such good handwriting. I can't read a word of this."

"I want you to read it."

This way he would have to come to terms with what she was feeling; though as she sat there all she felt was confusion.

"I feel like moving away," she said.

"What good would that do?" He was squinting at her writing. "Anyway, you wouldn't leave your poor old father alone in this dark old house – just me and the trees? Who would I talk to at night?"

"I don't know what to do."

After the third or fourth letter he pushed his chair back.

"You're saying the same thing, over and over. Now listen to me. All right, so you don't like the way it's turning out. It's not 100 per cent perfect, I know that. But has it been a mistake? I don't know. I'm apologising. I don't want a girl moping around as if it's the end of the world. But what is it you want? I'd say you don't know yourself. Am I right? This Mr Cave – Roy – you hardly know the man – he's not so bad. Anyway, I thought you took to him. At least you didn't screw your nose up. Have you spoken to him? I have been – a lot. I think there's a lot going on there. For starters, he's a

89

decent man; I think you would agree. He's a neat man, not a mess. He certainly knows a hell of a lot about trees."

"I've noticed."

Her father put his hand on her shoulder. "All we can do is wait and see."

Once outside she headed towards the river. "Where are you off to?" – her father's voice. She didn't know what was happening to her. As she walked quickly and entered the trees she stopped and in the stillness couldn't help touching, if only for a moment, the nearest of the evenly spaced trunks. Eucalypts which were the cause of it all also gave a moment's pause.

9

Maidenii

HERE IS THE tree Holland had given his daughter for her birthday. She was thirteen.

She'd come into his room early in undisguised anticipation; Holland couldn't help admiring her excitement. To extend the moment he did the cruel fatherly thing of frowning in feigned surprise, as if he didn't know what day it was. Then as doubts troubled Ellen's face he pointed to the wardrobe.

No amount of blue ribbon around the terracotta pot or explaining the exactness of the botanical name could disguise her disappointment. Instead of a gift she felt a loss. It was as if he was giving himself a present, and a very ordinary one. What could she do with a tree? Not even the ceremony of planting it together, on the northern slope facing the town, made her happier.

The years passed ordinarily enough. Gradually she had become less satisfied; she didn't know why. By the time the suitors began arriving in their trucks, cars, motorcycles, by train or on foot, Ellen returned to the lovely habit of wandering or simply being among the many different eucalypts. It was there one morning she remembered her tree, *E. maidenii*, and after several hours she located it at the far end of the property, where the soil was moist and rather heavy, a long way from the house.

Standing back Ellen smiled at what she saw.

It had grown as she had: slender, straight, pale. It was subtle in its limb-parting beauty; Ellen considered it female.

On impulse she felt like taking a broom and cleaning up the usual mess on the ground, sweeping the earth around the tree. Of all the eucalypts on the property this one belonged to her. And she wanted it to stand out, swept clean – the way a small-town war memorial is washed with soap and water.

At that moment, Ellen noticed a large rusty nail hammered into the trunk. It could only have been her father – who else? It gave a strange feeling. Not so much as if a nail had been driven into her; rather, vague surprise at seeing a steel object embedded in the softness of Nature. On the surrounding ground were no other human signs, no coil of fencing wire, or perforated beer can, or fading cigarette pack, shotgun cartridge near the rabbit holes.

The nail, at that moment, remained without a purpose.

It was a day humming with heat. Facing the tree, the way she faced a long mirror, she took her breasts, and lifted them gently from the pull of the earth. Vaguely she wanted to kiss herself. If the reddish earth, the dead leaves, dry twigs and grass, the ants and the remote and prickly eucalypts had not been uninviting, so unsympathetic, she would have undressed; taken everything off and faced the general warmth and wide-openness. She was that age.

* *

E. maidenii is related to Tasmania and the Southern Blue Gums (*E. globulus*); very vigorous trees.

The trunk has a short stocking of greyish bark at the base, the upper bark smooth, spotted. Its juvenile foliage is conspicuous and attractive in the undergrowth.

10

Torquata

STILL THE LANDSCAPE intrudes (not for much longer). An unpainted shearing shed floating on its shadow in a paddock, moored to the homestead by the slack line of a fence. It almost goes without saying the land is laced with wire. The straight line is immediately sharply human.

Oceans of swaying grasses – golden in summer, as mentioned before. It's often written that our crops and grasses sway and slap about like great oceans over the rounded earth; other times, a light breeze can curve the more sparsely planted stems to resemble golden hairs on a sailor's arm. Across a paddock in the afternoon: eucalypts repeated here and there on the ground by folding out at right angles, compressed as ink stains or thumb prints on a blotter. And always the scattered apparently random arrangements in Nature. It is this casual inevitability – the slant of the fallen tree breaking the verticals of others – that allows the eye to rest.

Ellen preferred the area around the old bridge, where the serene geometry of the eucalypts faintly raised the possibility she too was elegant – it was something like elegance; and the rustle of the nearby river in curve was a comfort, an alternative, as well.

Now that she had located her own tree she would occasionally visit it, around the other side of the hill.

Early one afternoon there she heard voices, men's, when none were expected. According to the rules laid down by Holland, a suitor could begin and end his test at any point on the property, and Mr Cave had suggested they switch to the bottom end for a change. Birds in advance began exploding from branches, some calling out warning, a rabbit, another, did their zigzag which attracts the gun, and a wallaby, rising, falling, close to Ellen.

She remained behind the pale tree when it would have been better to step out.

From halfway across the continent this man called Mr Cave was now advancing steadily towards her, to take her away. He was the one. The eucalypts here were congested. That didn't stop him. Without altering his voice he identified each and every species in passing, Holland murmuring assent, until they were standing quite close.

On this day Mr Cave wore a collar and tie, and a sweat patch had spread on his back into the shape of Papua New Guinea, while Holland's face was pale red, a coralfish passing through trees. They were talking about snakes, sizes of, where seen, how almost stepped on, etc. Snake stories vary only in length from man to man.

"They get into your sleeping bag for warmth," said Cave. "That's been known to happen."

"As well as all the eucalypts, we've got the most venomous snakes!"

"So I'm told."

They were around the other side of the tree. It was too late for Ellen to step out and surprise them.

"Sea snakes, I hope I never come across one of them. Soap Mallee, and the tall one is *kirtoni*. Now that's what I call a eucalypt. That could go on a postcard tomorrow. *Maidenii*, am I right? Always a favourite of mine."

Her father's shadow nodded.

"And you'd have to travel a long way to see a better specimen, if I do say so myself."

At this moment, almost forgetting her position, Ellen looked on at the casual surface-manner of men. These two were now searching around inside their trousers, and Mr Cave's hand, the nearest, came out in full view with a soft thing, its lidded eye surveying Ellen; they began pissing, Mr Cave, her father, against the trunk.

All she could decide and so remain puzzled by was how their behaviour was indifferently at odds to hers. Side by side they remained looking down at themselves, and up at the trees. To Ellen it somehow followed on from the way Mr Cave fanned out across the landscape like a cone or searchlight, consuming all before him; and before long he would be consuming her.

Hiding behind the trunk Ellen felt weakened. She also felt irritated. As they finished, she could hear one of them breathing.

Now awaiting discovery Ellen shut her eyes; though it was not to be, not yet.

11

Nubilis

ANOTHER SUITOR WITH impressive credentials stepped forward only to be told to stand aside until Mr Cave was finished.

He had a ginger beard, and his name was Swingle. Working behind a desk at the Botanic Gardens in Melbourne he had been dismissed for taking unauthorised field trips; for his ambition was to discover an unknown eucalypt species, even a subspecies, in order to have it named after him, the way others have left a trace of themselves in the names of butterflies, roses, ferns – and of course eucalypts. If Miss Mary Merrick of the Royal Botanic Gardens in Sydney was rewarded for her long years in the library with *E. merrickiae*, better known as the Goblet Mallee, why couldn't he? A certain Mr H. S. Bloxsome had a species named after him because it happened to be found on his property in south-eastern Queensland . . .

Swingle's simple quest for immortality had taken him into remote and difficult terrain. On one of these solitary trips he had broken an arm. Recently on a ledge in the Grampians he had trodden on and destroyed the only remaining plant of an unknown dwarf eucalypt with extremely narrow leaves. He did it, and he didn't know it.

Curiously he was a modest man. And as his life dream became less and less likely Swingle became, as they say, *merely philosophical* – that is rueful, not embittered.

The scientific naming of trees doesn't follow a pattern. In some respects it has an attractive, amateur randomness just like the distribution of the trees themselves. Some names are descriptive of bark, leaves and so on; towns and mountain ranges close to a eucalypt's habitat become lengthened and *latinised*; explorers and a few tree-interested politicians have left their mark; many professional and amateur plant collectors, and a few watercolour artists, are honoured. The Reverend E. N. McKie, a Presbyterian minister at Guyra, was one enthusiast, specialising in stringybarks – McKie's Stringybark (*E. mckieana*).

Very often it is the common name that is instantly evocative: Leather Jacket, Weeping Gum, Ghost Gum, Coolibah to name some.

How did *E. nubilis* get its name? A curious one. *Nubilis* means "marriageable".

12

Baxteri

THE STORY IS not at all uncommon or unusual.

It was told to Ellen by a man she met only days before (so, a virtual stranger), who had a circuitous story-telling manner, as if he was making it up, and what is more he told it under a tree where the crows were making their din; he also added bits of factual information she had no way of verifying, which seemed to have little bearing on the main thing being said. For all these distractions Ellen found the story powerful for what it may have represented, in other words, for what it didn't say exactly.

A young man, he said, travelled from Great Britain to Bombay where he booked into the most famous hotel in India, the Taj Mahal, which had been designed by his great-grandfather at the end of the last century. He wanted to see with his own eyes whether it had been tragically positioned in relation to the sea. It faces, or appears to, the Gateway of India, and the sea there is as brown every day of the year as the people who stand gazing at it. In his family the story was told how their great-grandfather designed the hotel down to the door knobs and the depth of the skirting boards, and defended each and every detail of the design as if his life depended on it. Somehow he managed to retain the incredibly extravagant staircase and the domineering dome that seemed to have no other function than to make this hotel look like an opera house or the stock exchange. A large part of an architect's genius is in the winning of the argument. Satisfied, the architect left by boat on home leave.

No one knows what happened to him in London. Something happened. Inevitably, there was talk of a woman.

Instead of four months he stayed away eighteen months. When he returned to Bombay his great project was almost completed. He took one look at it and found the local builders had positioned the huge building back to front: it was not facing the sea! The story then, as handed down, was that he literally tore his hair out and, in an act of protest and unimaginable disappointment, threw himself from the top of the semicircular staircase, and died.

The architect's great-grandson introduced himself to the hotel's management. Although they would neither confirm nor deny the rumour surrounding the architect's death he was given a room overlooking the sea, at a generous discount. He ventured out onto the streets. About his own career he was undecided. For a few days he was ill. Otherwise his visit was . . . inconclusive.

We now pick up the trail on our own doorstep. Instead of returning to Great Britain the young man flew to Sydney, and after spending a few days on the beach made his way to Bathurst.

Bathurst? The coldest country town in New South Wales? He was however an historically minded person; he personified Englishness. And Bathurst was the western-most point reached by Charles Darwin in eighteen-hundred-something. There's a plaque that says this in the municipal gardens.

So there he is in Bathurst, our traveller from Britain.

It is at Bathurst or, rather, on the outskirts, that the story develops a sudden twist. On the second day he was wandering along the river when he came across two brown snakes – one shedding its skin. He killed the wrong one, and was turned into a woman. That's apparently what happened.

When last heard of he was living in Seattle – or was it San Francisco? – as a woman.

The court building in Bathurst is so extravagant it looks out of place. In the early days, designs for the colony's civic buildings came from Whitehall. It is said that Bathurst was sent by mistake plans for a court building in an Indian city, while the Indian city received the more modest court building which would have done for Bathurst.

But that's another story.

13

Microtheca

E LLEN WATCHED AS Mr Cave stumbled. For a moment he looked finished; but as befitting a monarch he remained calm. Idly he looked away from the tree in question, a maddeningly nondescript mallee, obstinately modest, one barely surviving – the shrubby *E. fruticosa*, it's easily confused with *E. foecunda*.

He began talking about something altogether different, namely how to fix the problem in this driest of continents of the rivers that flow as quickly as they possibly can into the sea, an oversight in nature that has produced a vast dead centre, an area of absurd emptiness, useless for just about everything, except to encourage millions of poor-quality photographs and to exercise the imaginations of politicians, journalists and other lateral thinkers. Ellen, who had just delivered a thermos of tea, noticed his sentences were trailing, and that he was stealing glances at the foliage.

Then he stopped talking. For Mr Cave – and for Ellen waiting – it extended into a crucial minute or more.

It was Ellen who began to fret. She wanted to close her eyes, anything to encourage the possibility of release.

He pulled off a leaf.

"A eucalypt with no common name," his back still turned. And in a voice of suppressed eagerness, which has its source in the national quiz shows, he gave the correct name, in Latin.

After that Ellen couldn't watch any more, and without a word went down to the river. In and out ran her thoughts, as if she was actually running through the trees: marriage by arrangement; more her father's than hers; marriage at arm's length; without-her-consent marriage, without her participation; her entire self given to him, from Adelaide; a blank marriage; nothing more. And her father, it seemed, always spoke to her in a deliberately light, often bantering way.

The stillness of the trees had a calming effect. Yet she almost let out an animal cry of some kind, in despair.

And as the evenly spaced trunks multiplied on both sides and behind, she felt vague pleasure at the notion she was "running away" from them, the two men.

Silver light slanted into the motionless trunks, as if coming from narrow windows. The cathedral has taken its cue from the forest. The vaulted roof soaring to the heavens, pillars in smooth imitation of trees, even the obligatory echo, are calculated to make a person feel small, and so trigger feelings of obscure wonder. In cathedral and forest making even a scraping noise would trample soft feelings. For this reason, Ellen unconsciously continued on tiptoe.

Where the mathematics ended and opened into light and space Ellen decided to turn, when something on the ground under a tree caught her eye. For a moment she thought it was a bundle of clothing her father had left there. Soft contours of flesh come forward in bush, the trees and undergrowth suddenly act as backdrops.

It was a man, lying in the shade; a foreign body, on their property.

She thought: another suitor!

On the point of marching back to the house she took instead another two steps. For a few minutes she remained very still, and nothing around her moved. What if he was dead? She took a few steps more. If he was asleep she would see who he was. She wanted to see his face.

But his head was half-buried in one elbow. Both were drenched in shade. To see his face Ellen hesitated, then squatted.

She was close enough to touch him.

He hadn't shaved. A tanned jaw. He'd been out in the weather. A wanderer. What appeared to be a swag alongside was hard and narrow, a worn black case, the kind used to hold scientific instruments, not musical. In these parts his hair would be considered long. To Ellen it was Sydney hair. His clothes too were carelessly worn, of good quality.

As Ellen watched, his lips moved. "He must be dreaming." And, "What would a man out here, under a tree, dream about, or someone like him be thinking about?"

Concerning the bodies of men, the visible areas: they have the scars. Men tend to accumulate them. Scars are *worn* by men, almost as women wear jewellery. To carry a scar is to carry a story. The very suggestion can extend a person. Beneath every scar, then – a story, unfortunately.

Ellen was looking at the short transparent mark below the eye, a completely straight tear, when the eye itself opened, and considered her.

Green-khaki was the eye. Under the circumstances, riddled as they were with chance – and harsh light and filtered shade – it was the eye colour Ellen expected.

Yet he remained not moving, not even shifting the elbow. It was as if – on their land – he was lying in bed.

To her surprise she spoke first. "What is it you want?"

"Who might you be?"

"That doesn't matter!" Ellen stood up. He was being smart. Brushing imaginary twigs and leaves off her loose cotton dress she thought about going. Now he sat up. He was older than she was, though nothing like as old as her father or Mr Cave. He may have been thirty-three, no more.

"I opened my eyes just then, and instead of stars I saw . . . spots before me."

Ellen wasn't sure what he was talking about. She made as if to go. "You were talking in your sleep."

"That's not as interesting as it sounds. What did I say?"

"It was someone's name."

He laughed: and remained that way, angled up at the overhead branches, the drooping leaves. "What is this tragic-looking tree? I should have chosen a better one. Unless I'm mistaken, it's a –"

As it happens *E. microtheca*, well known as Coolibah, was one of the very few eucalypts Ellen recognised, only because her father had often poked fun at its shocking historical significance, the "history of shallow graves", as he put it.

But the stranger never actually named the tree.

Perhaps he wasn't another suitor on the loose after all. Frowning, she recalled her father every other day warning about men and the way they used words. So far this one had hardly said a thing. When she stole a glance he wasn't even looking in her direction. He had his carved head turned, absorbed in something else.

It was too much that he should sit there as he pleased! At the same time Ellen felt a faintly spreading comfort at the way they each allowed without difficulty a silence to open between them. No sooner had this registered than she felt annoyed, and wanted it to show, without quite knowing why.

"Why not sit down? Either that or I'll get to my feet. I can't have you towering over me. It doesn't make sense."

Without waiting he stood up anyway, which encouraged from Ellen a faint smile.

Again he looked away.

"Do you know . . . " He moved about, hands in pockets; for no apparent reason, he gave a sort of Irish jig which almost had Ellen laughing – as if he, complete stranger, was pleased to see her.

It was enough to make her want to leave, except he was telling her something, even though he had his back turned.

There he was pulling off a strip of bark. When he turned shadows fluttered and flowed over his face like feathers or water.

"Do you know . . . " he began, "there is a woman who lives in Melbourne, not far from the River Yarra. For many years she worked for a firm of solicitors in Bourke Street, specialising in wills."

Clearing his throat he glanced at Ellen, a few paces away.

"She was born in Eastern Europe, in a city of many bridges. Her father had a dark moustache and hair very crinkled and grey. His hair must have been like a creek or your river here in flood. He wore his coat over his shoulders, as the men in his city still do . . . That's an odd habit, almost feminine, don't you think? This woman first realised her father was a tenor of renown when he took her as a child on a picnic and sang in a pine forest. Her mother was a singer, too. She came from a prosperous old merchant family.

"Yes, in that country there was the repressive political system. It's government by *cement*. No one could leave this country without permission. And even if they did manage to get permission they couldn't take money out. It was worthless. To get around this people tried all kinds of creative methods.

"Under a tree in the garden the woman's parents had buried a valuable stamp collection of the nineteenth-century classics, rare items from Cape of Good Hope, Mauritius and Tasmania. It had been inherited from someone on the mother's side. Every year or so the tenor with the moustache would go to the tree, dig out the enam-elled tin wrapped in oilcloth and, with a pair of tweezers" – here he fixed one eye on Ellen – "remove a *single precious stamp* which they would then easily slip into an envelope and sell in Geneva for hard currency. It was how they continued their singing tours in Europe.

"The father always spoiled his daughter. He always returned with extravagant presents for her. When he went to cafés with his men friends he sometimes took her. With them he was boisterous. Sometimes she fell asleep with her hand in his pocket. A few times he introduced her to beautifully dressed women who never seemed to stop laughing – some wearing hats with veils, and who left lipstick on white cakes and glasses.

"By now she had grown into a young woman. Yes, we would have to say she had a melancholy beauty. A red-haired law student had no doubts at all. But they could only whisper to each other in the street or at the café. Her father wouldn't have him near the house, or let him see her. At the mention of his name he'd fly into a rage. As far as her father was concerned he didn't have a single thing going for him. To make matters worse the student was under surveillance for certain political activity.

"He was told not to bother writing any letters. Anything he wrote would be intercepted by the father and burnt."

Half in sunlight, Ellen was searching his face to see if he was making it up as he went along.

He continued the story, taking his time.

"There were a few stamps left. To take her mind off the student who, he discovered, was meeting his daughter in secret he took her away on a trip, just the two of them. They went first to Switzerland – to cash a stamp. In Geneva he met an Italian diva. What a prima donna – straight out of the textbooks! The daughter looked on as her father fell for her. He wouldn't give up till she was his. The daughter was with her father as he followed the diva across Europe. At last, in a five-star hotel in Madrid, he succeeded. Almost at the same time he ran out of money! They had to return home. Weeping and resting his head on his daughter's breast he sang mournful songs in the train.

"His stout wife was waiting for them with her arms folded. One look at him was enough. It was the same story all over again. There was always another woman somewhere. This time she decided to do nothing.

"But there was little now he had to say to his wife. He had thoughts only for the Italian prima donna. He lost his appetite. He couldn't sleep. He decided to leave again for Switzerland, this time alone. The wife suddenly tried to intervene. She struggled, she wept. She begged her daughter to help. The daughter, who now lives in Melbourne – he always listened to what she said. And they were so alike. Meanwhile the red-haired student had been arrested. It was jail, he was told, or leave the country.

"The daughter struck a bargain with her father: they would share the remaining stamps. She would leave with the student, while he could join the prima donna.

"The father readily agreed."

While talking, this stranger appeared to notice something in the sky. He narrowed his eyes.

"Together they chose a day to leave." His voice sounded interested in the heat. "The daughter went out of her way to be nice to her mother, but the mother wouldn't have it. Those enclosed countries, naturally they produce distortions. At the Dig-Tree she joined her father on his knees as he felt around for the tin containing the stamps. There was something childlike about his optimism – he was humming a hopeful aria. To think that a few images on perforated paper in the palm of a hand could hold the solution to their lives.

"She remembered the wink he gave. It was necessary to keep quiet.

"Only an hour before she'd been using the philatelic tweezers to pluck her eyebrows. Now she held them ready as he opened the enamelled tin. The coat fell off his shoulders.

"The stamps had all been burnt. Nothing remained in the tin but ashes.

"Years later she managed to leave the country, choosing a place as far away as possible. The others in this story, including the student, remained behind, occasionally recognising each other."

Poor, poor woman, Ellen thought. And Ellen tried to picture her, the daughter, now a woman living in Melbourne – a long, long way from her own country. How could the father have continued? Together in the house with the mother? A story never ends, she could see. In any life the neat finish cannot be. It is only the beginning.

She wanted to know more. But the stranger, he wasn't interested. Evidently now he was thinking about something else. The way he had turned away, leaving her there as if she was merely a tree, nothing more . . . it was incredibly rude. There was no one else within a mile of them. Now even his noticeably long hair and, for that matter, his settled eyes, were quite out of place, in the glare.

Ready to let him know by walking off she saw to her amazement he seemed to be wandering away, or half-wandering, leaving her under the Coolibah. They each left the tree. Ellen had no interest in seeing him again.

14

Camaldulensis

S o   c o m m o n   w e r e   some eucalypts they hardly
deserved Mr Cave's attention. Now and then Holland
had to call him back and repeat the ground rules, which had
been carefully explained in the beginning – the way a
referee calls the contenders in a heavyweight title fight to
the centre of the ring, looking up at one man then the other,
the trainers joining in with vacant expressions as they
massage the necks of their fighters – and the rules were that
every single eucalypt had to be named if he, or anybody else
for that matter, was to win the hand of his daughter. Now
let's get moving.

Still, it can be admitted that almost anything can be
taken for granted. And it is true that certain eucalypts
pass before the eyes in such lavish quantities they undergo
a sort of optical *browning*, and actually become invisible
with ordinariness, as is the fate of weeds and telegraph
poles.

Ellen had been told to watch out for the unexpected
behind the ordinary. Each and every object in the world has
its own history, it goes without saying, which is a result of
some other history, and so on; forever continuing. It can be

triggered, Ellen was told, by a name. And the unexpected can appear in small and large lumps.

The most common eucalypt in the world is the Red Gum. Hundreds on Holland's property alone followed the river. And yet – small example of the unexpected – for all its widespread distribution, it has not been found in Tasmania.

Over time the River Red Gum (*E. camaldulensis*) has become barnacled with legends. This is only to be expected. By sheer numbers there's always a bulky Red Gum here or somewhere else in the wide world, muscling into the eye, as it were; and by following the course of rivers in our particular continent they don't merely imprint their fuzzy shape but actually worm their way greenly into the mind, giving some hope against the collective crow-croaking dryness. And if that's not enough the massive individual squatness of these trees, ancient, stained and warty, has a grandfatherly aspect; that is, a long life of incidents, seasons, stories.

Curiously, for all its wide distribution in Australia, the River Red Gum was first described in the literature from a cultivated tree in the walled garden of the Camalduli religious order in Naples. How did this happen?

Ellen was given a few parts of the story (almost like the keel of an unfinished ship); enough for her to inhabit, to give voices and faces. In her journal she scribbled possible explanations.

Late in the nineteenth century a paddle-steamer captain – Irish, a widower, based in Wentworth – vowed to kill his own daughter!

This man was much sought after in the river trade. He had an uncanny knack of navigating the Darling River, long into the summer months. He was a familiar sight at the wheel, unsmiling, his daughter alongside, smiling and waving. One day it was noticed she was no longer there. Almost immediately his times slowed, and he began running aground, once loaded with wool bales. As he continued piloting the river it wasn't the loss of business that troubled him, but suspicions of his daughter's behaviour, suspicions which were always aggravated by the sight at Wentworth of the Darling River flowing into and becoming one with the stronger Murray River. Unless he was mistaken his daughter's appearance had subtly altered.

As it happened his suspicions were justified. Not yet twenty his daughter was seeing a local grazier's son. The whole town knew. She had become pregnant. The couple fled the day before he returned from his weekly river trip. He set out to follow. He was not even interested in bringing her back.

Years later and now with a large ginger moustache he traced her to the Camaldulensians in Naples, a contemplative order that practises silence, fasting and manual labour.

He was directed to a broad woman scratching with a hoe. After travelling across the world the poor man stood rubbing his eyes. It was her coarse garment, and placid expression; she seemed to be in a dream. The child had been taken away.

He began questioning her.

What happened then is almost too fleeting to record. Either in anger or relief or to get a word out of her – nobody knows – he took her by the shoulders. They struggled in the garden, kicking up dust; swaying and locked together, Ellen heard it told.

It was then, *the story goes*, a Red Gum seed dormant in the river man's trouser cuff spilled onto the ground.

It could even be – in fact, it would appear to be the only explanation – that the ceremonial struggle between the father and daughter on that particular spot on the earth foot-scuffed and kicked the seed into the barren soil. For soon after he left, shaking and exhausted, a green shoot appeared.

The daughter tended it until it grew into a healthy sapling, and she lived with the Camalduli order long enough to see the sapling become a tree, then a full-grown River Red Gum, a tree of great girth, dominating the garden, its water-seeking roots cracking walls and sucking dry the vegetable plots, the same tree that lined for hour after hour the Darling River, which she would never again see.

15

Planchoniana

ELLEN REMAINED INDOORS. At about nine-thirty she made tea for her father and Mr Cave, one with dirty fingernails, the other clean, and after they set off and their voices, littered with latinised names, placenames and occasional surnames remained in the air before dying, a vast stillness descended on the land and the homestead; it filled the hollows and every part of a room; certainly not only water finds its own level.

Then returning to her room Ellen had plenty of things to record or discuss in her journal. It was there she returned to her encounter with the man asleep. These were hot days as she studied her nakedness in the mirror. And she drifted off east to Sydney, to its city edge – crowds, glare of white, the blue-green. In Sydney she could simply be amongst many others, other women, taking part in a constant overlapping sliding motion, joining them (without necessarily knowing any of them). Later in the morning there was housework; moving about, busying herself, she let her thoughts drift. That in slow combination was how she spent her days.

In the front room, as she darned her father's socks, the

needle pierced her little finger. Her head flew back like an irritated horse.

She tasted the blood, then wrapped the finger in a handkerchief. She soon changed handkerchiefs. The finger wouldn't stop bleeding.

Mr Cave stood before her – those pleats, his body heat. So he'd notched up another successful day in the field.

He held out a gumnut.

"For you," he said, "I picked it up on the way down. It makes an ideal thimble."

Ellen smiled. For the first time he'd decided to look at her. Head bowed she tried the gum nut. It fitted. "I thought it would," he said. Fat men make the finest dancers, she had been told. Very gently he was undoing the handkerchief.

"Do you have any molasses in the kitchen? Stick your finger in it. It'll sting like blazes, but it will stop the bleeding. It was a trick my mother picked up. She was from the country."

From the other room her father was yelling out to him.

"Your father wants to show me something."

Absently slipping the gum nut on the pricked finger Ellen saw that Mr Cave's sudden approach to her was a sign of his practical side. He knew he would be winning her; any day now. He could hardly take her away cold, as it were. Meanwhile, the bleeding had stopped. It was the gum nut. Ellen wanted to point this out to Mr Cave. At that time she was all too ready to assign meanings to casual events.

"Anyway," he virtually smiled, "ask your father for the short common name of *planchoniana*."

16

Approximans

A ND THERE ARE stories (it was explained) that consist of such slender means it's a wonder they can be called stories at all. These are the ones tossed off in a line or two: fragments, with no ending – too factual. They are approximately stories, or possibly stories. They are more like sums. Such brevity goes against the iron law offered by the celebrated German colossus: "All good stories are slow stories."

Still it cannot be denied that the briefest anecdote (there, we won't say "story") can produce an echo of really curious, indelible power. For the same reason, let us not forget, artists give high value to drawings and thumbnail sketches.

In Rangoon after the war a once-grand hotel, which is still operating to this day, had a Beale piano in the dining room. The Beale is an Australian-made piano. It has a *eucalyptus lid*. And in the clatter and murmur of the dining room, under the whirring of ceiling fans, or probably because it was the cabaret custom anyway, the piano lid was always raised. It hardly mattered that the Beale, made in Sydney, was usually out of tune.

Planters' wives, traders, government officers liked to dress up and, in the tremendous humidity, dance to waltzes and foxtrots played on the Beale, one or two violins accompanying. Piano, violins and humidity: infinite melancholy.

The flow of sound released via the raised eucalyptus lid of the Beale would have produced a secondary, more lasting echo between more than a few couples – the complications, the distinct possibilities; so many different stories would have grown around chosen people, and hovered like musical notes, thanks to the Beale with its raised lid. The solitary piano in Rangoon or even the lid itself would have become the source or the core of a story or many stories. "If you see what I mean," he said.

17

Imlayensis

POSSIBLY THE RAREST of all eucalypts, the Mount Imlay Mallee has been seen by – rough estimate – a few dozen lucky people. Only about seventy plants are supposed to be in existence, all in the one small area among rocks near the summit of Mount Imlay, on the far south coast of New South Wales. Young trunks are green, the colour of dragonflies or parrots, until they weather to orange-brown or grey.

How Holland managed to obtain a seedling remains a mystery. The world of eucalypts can be viciously protective; stories of ignorance and betrayal spread like bushfires, and are just as difficult to stamp out. People in the field never quite knew what to make of Holland. He wasn't really one of them. It was hard though not to respect his tenacity.

Still more impressive was how he managed to cultivate on his property, so far inland, a Mount Imlay Mallee.

From the tower Ellen watched the two distant figures toiling across a paddock as if against a headwind. At intervals they were blotted out by a cultivated tree. They were heading as the crow flies for the outcrop of quartzite at the southern end where the rarest of eucalypts had taken root; she knew because her father had winked and nodded at her over breakfast. But the very rarity of the Mount Imlay Mallee gave it such a distinctive appearance it would make identification easy, at least for someone of Mr Cave's calibre.

Ellen lowered her head when they disappeared. She couldn't have kept looking anyway. Every tree Mr Cave went towards was another step towards her. In this way her father appeared as some sort of usher. He was driving her away. In the tower it was warm. Ellen turned her attention to her toes and as she examined her knee recalled the other suitors, their voices, hopeful faces. For an hour or more she seemed to gaze at her knee. It was several days since she had come across the sleeping man. It wasn't his hair Ellen thought about now, but his manner, which was perplexing. The suddenness of it all was almost irritating, she scribbled in her journal.

When she looked up again and across the tree-dotted paddock – the direction opposite to Mr Cave and her father – she could just make out near a denser clump of trees a single figure, moving.

Such a sight was rare on their place. It looked like him, the man of medium build she'd found asleep on the ground. She hurried down the narrow steps into the wide-open light, and strolling, but with firmness, reached the approximate spot.

No sign of him, just eucalypts here and there, which in her restlessness looked all the same. To Ellen, her life was like this. As supplied by her father it had casual abundance, shown by the trees, and an unresolved puzzle at its centre.

As for the green blouse she normally wore only on special occasions it somehow added impatience to her speckled beauty.

18

Foecunda

AFTER MANY ADVENTURES along many roads – many cities, towns and forests – he had arrived at Holland's property tired, at the beginning of summer. He was alert, and a hard one to pin down; he was indifferent to a lot of things. Illness had made him thoughtful. Otherwise he might have seemed irresponsible.

And instead of returning early in the morning to the far long paddock Ellen went among the darker trunks by the river, in view of the road.

It was a form of drifting; almost like fishing.

She'd only paused for a minute near the still water by the bridge when someone whistled at her. Instead of hostile dismissal, as in town, she turned.

"Oh, you're still here . . . I thought you'd left our district."

"District," he repeated. He stood more or less facing her. "Apart from that, what have you been doing?"

"I look after my father."

"He needs looking after?"

"Probably not."

"I imagine it's sometimes hard to know." He had his arms folded, but not harshly.

"He is my father," she wanted to say. "And you don't know him."

"A bite of apple?"

The lure of sharing food, and of clean spherical dimensions which show the amount taken, is irresistible. And as Ellen reached out, her sleeve slid back and laid bare her arm.

"I saw someone like you yesterday from the house."

But he had taken a male bite from the apple and only appeared to nod. The way his jaws worked reminded her of a horse. They were heading through the different trees to the end of the long paddock anyway.

"How many eucalypts do you suppose are here?"

"I think even my father's lost count. He's got them all written down."

"Obviously we're talking about hundreds."

They came to the outburst of imprecise bushes normally found in a sandy band along the bottom of Australia.

"About here," Ellen turned and faced the house. "I think it was you . . . about there."

"Of all the eucalypts, the mallees leave me cold. They can never make up their minds which direction to take."

He gave a sly look of complicity which she couldn't, at that stage, accept.

"Don't the mallees leave you cold? Don't you prefer a good old solid gum tree, the kind," he said hopefully, "you see on calendars?"

"I'm not interested in any of them!"

The subject was the least interesting she could think of. The only people who came to the property were men hoping to please her father, all wearing their ridiculous detailed knowledge of trees. The very word *eucalyptus*, which many would swear is the loveliest of all words, was for Ellen an unbearable word, a bearer of troubles. Anyone who entered the world of eucalypts came out narrowed and reduced, was her opinion. And now this one standing beside her pulling off a leaf, he was surely another one. Although he didn't exactly come out with the species' name, the Narrow-leafed Mallee (*E. foecunda*), he seemed to know, for he glanced at it and cleared his throat.

There was an Italian, he said, who had a fruit shop in Carlton.

This man, he continued, was the first in Melbourne to call himself a FRUITOLOGIST – if you've ever wondered where that came from – and have it painted in green letters outside his shop. His fruit was the best quality. He lived above the shop. Both parents had died. He was a hunch-back. Not a severe hunchback, but enough to pull his mouth down a little on one side. Everybody liked him. He was careful to listen to women. In turn they wouldn't hear a word said against him, let alone his fruit, though they would also shake their heads and laugh at any suggestion of marriage.

His shop in Carlton was famous for its displays of fruit. These he composed with great patience and skill each Sunday, behind the shutters. He had plenty of colours and shapes to choose from.

The usual pyramids of apples and so on he dismissed as too common. Instead he did detailed maps of Italy using green and yellow peppers, or the state of Queensland to celebrate the mango season. National flags, football of course, clocks and a cyclist were some of his memorable subjects. As his skills increased he turned to fruit sculptures: these included nativity scenes; an Ayers Rock of Tasmanian apples; anti-war scenes using cantaloupes; custard apples and pineapples.

It was his hobby, which also happened to be good for business. People would ask, "So what have you dreamed up for us this week?"

The care and attention the hunchback lavished on his fresh fruit displays had begun modestly enough as something to stave off that peculiar atmosphere of desolation "which pervades Anglo-Saxon towns on Sundays". At the same time it gave pleasure to customers or people passing on the footpath. Gradually the displays grew in ambition and complexity, demanding on his part still more patience, ingenuity and stamina – to name just a few of the requirements. While the hunchback continued serving as always quietly in his shop, the fruit sculptures became more extreme.

Working next door in the cakeshop was a young woman. Occasionally she stepped into his shop – to buy a bunch of grapes, or something. Whenever she passed he paused to look at her. Never once did she so much as glance in the hunchback's direction, let alone acknowledge his presence, even when he happened to be standing on the footpath in his apron.

He gave her some grapes once; she took them with barely a thankyou. And, it goes without saying, she didn't take the slightest interest in his fruit displays, which as a consequence became more and more ambitious.

Now this young woman had extraordinary blue eyes which belonged more to a Persian cat (a distilled version of the blurry blue of the mountains west of Sydney). Even more extraordinary, and perhaps connected to the colour of her eyes, was the way at every opportunity she looked at herself – not only in mirrors, but in windows, doors, bonnets of cars, puddles. It didn't matter whether she was in the middle of walking or talking to someone. At every opportunity she tried to catch a glimpse of herself. Often as she noticed her reflection she used it to adjust hair and clothing. She couldn't help it. Here was self-absorption developed into a tic.

Was she lovely or was she beautiful? Ellen wondered about the blue eyes.

Lovely or beautiful, it doesn't really matter. She had long, straightish hair and a slightly empty expression. The poor hunchback became obsessed with her. To have her to himself would make his life complete.

At every spare moment – even when serving customers – he considered ways to catch her attention.

He sat down and drew up a list. Colours were sifted. He calculated quantities. Special orders were placed for exotic fruits. At the market he personally selected each item and weighed it by hand, looking for shape as well as evenness of colour.

All Sunday he worked behind the closed front of the shop. And he was still at it, making finishing touches, in the morning. He was like those earnest birds in New Guinea that busily collect bottle tops and bits of glass in their nests to attract the female.

The usual bystanders and early customers gathered, and when he raised the shutters, a politician unveiling a bronze, a murmur of admiration rustled among them.

It had passed the first test.

All he had to do now was wait.

Some tourists were taking photographs; children jumped up and down and pointed at it. A customer who lectured in art history at the nearby university began congratulating him, "A masterpiece. And I am not one who uses that word lightly . . . "

At that moment she appeared, in high heels. He left a customer in mid-sentence and moved to the front.

Hurrying late for work she still managed to glance left and right for any reflective surfaces. And yet – what's this? – she walked straight past his window without noticing anything special. He hung around waiting. Mid-morning she passed again without noticing; at lunchtime too; and again on her way home when her attention was caught not by his fruit sculpture but by the side mirror of his parked truck.

There she was, modelled in the window, head on bare shoulders, an amazingly faithful Arcimboldian mosaic: her peaches and cream complexion; sliced apple and dates for nose; forehead of pawpaw; banana chin; glistening teeth of pomegranate; eyebrows, kiwifruit; juicy plum lips; bunches of guavas did for ears; pears formed her shoulders; and other bits and pieces too subtle immediately to recognise but contributing to the whole. With a split in the forehead and delicate placement of nectarines and figs he had even captured her self-obsession.

It was all there, in loving accuracy – except for the eyes. He had been unable to find a light blue fruit. Without the eyes she apparently couldn't see herself.

And he accidentally brushed against Ellen as he reached over to rest the flat of his hand against a splendid smooth trunk, which happened to be a Southern Blue Gum (*E. bicostata*).

19

Sideroxylon

WHY DID THE lovesick grocer have to be a hunchback? As if he didn't have enough problems, living alone above the shop, etc.

It was only a story. It is necessary for the story.

He should never have called himself a "fruitologist" – a bad sign, as far as Ellen was concerned.

When the stranger had left the story dangling in mid-air, she felt a sudden impatience at his indifference to her questions, such as, "Did she eventually stop in front of the shop and recognise herself? And then what? Couldn't someone tell her? And shoes – what sort of shoes did she wear?"

Instead, he moved on to the next tree, a squat *angry-looking* eucalypt near the pale brown dam, which seemed to remind him of another, entirely different story. Ellen searched his face. Was he making it up as he went along?

The tree was a Mugga Ironbark (*E. sideroxylon*).

This is not a happy story.

In one of the countless culs-de-sac in Canberra lived a retired public servant and his wife. For the last seventeen years they had only spoken to each other through their dog.

"Will the old bitch get off her backside and make a cup of tea?"

"He can make his own, I've been serving the so-and-so for all these years."

Ellen began laughing.

This is supposed to be an unhappy story!

During his working life the man had climbed the many levels of the public service until he was responsible for all the weights and measures in Australia. It was a career that had resulted in a certain satisfaction. After all, it had demonstrated how one thing inevitably follows another: coming down hard on sloppy standards of weights and measures produced a corresponding rise in career-trajectory. In turn, it encouraged in his private life a high degree of precision and disappointment.

"I left some toast on the table for him, I hope it goes cold."

"Always in the old dressing gown, isn't she? You'd think she'd look at herself in the mirror."

Each waited impatiently for the other's death; in the meantime they each did their best to win over the dog, a slow-moving kelpie, patting and feeding it the choicest scraps from their plates, all the time talking to and through it. As the kelpie grew even more slow-moving they became afraid of how they would address each other if it died.

The woman was the first to go. Busy with the crossword the husband had not noticed anything different. She was discovered on the bedroom floor around lunchtime; the man heard the dog making a faint noise.

From that day on the kelpie stayed close to the man.

The house felt more than half-empty.

Every Tuesday and Friday he went to her grave, the slow-moving dog following, and complained to her about the dog, while it lay at his feet: what the dog did; what it didn't do; the mess it made in the laundry; its fleas; how it didn't respond to his whistle any more.

And then after a few months, in what could only be described as the worst possible result, the man woke in the morning to find the acquiescent dog too had died.

Agreed, it was an unhappy story. Ellen wanted to tell him and at the same time ask if he liked dogs. She had suddenly many questions; but he had moved to another tree, seemingly at random, a Grey Gum (*E. punctata*), which is called Leather Jacket on account of its bark, and eased into virtually an identical story – except for one crucial difference.

As follows: a shoemaker in Leichhardt (I should tell you it's a suburb in Sydney of telegraph poles and telegraph wires and red telephones) every evening goes to the grave of his wife, often forgetting to take off his leather apron, and tells her the news of the day, and asks her advice, "Mrs Cudlipp's heels have gone again, those green shoes. She should take off weight. I forgot to water the flowers. We're running out of laces again. You know the Farini girl, the one whose boyfriend picks her up on the motorbike? He came a cropper, and tore his leather jacket. 'I only do shoes,' I told her. I took a look, I can patch it up. What do I charge? The usual? The postman, Reg, he's back again. Of course his tips keep falling off. I've told him a thousand times, rubber, switch to rubber, as you always said. But he's the old school.

He likes his cup of tea! Two women are going to the same wedding, you know them. My memory's going. Both high heels, reinforcement of the straps. The one with the loud voice, you said her mother was deaf. Man came in for change for a parking meter. Did I tell you the lease is up in November? I did, yes. We'll have to nut that one out, I've got a few thoughts. They say it's going to rain tomorrow."

He also wanted to know what to do with all her shoes, sensible shoes, with affectionate wrinkles, which remained in rows at the bottom of their wardrobe.

This story which had rolled off his tongue was supposed to be an antidote to the one about the stagnation of a marriage, the bitter canine catastrophe, as he put it; but Ellen found it sad, far sadder, almost too sad to contemplate. As she pondered the strengths and weaknesses of a long companionship, the trees around her went out of focus; it was all verging on a dream. The subject of course was as vast and as varied as a forest, the different aspects coming in from different angles in different shades.

Glancing, she wondered how he'd look in a leather jacket.

To cheer her up, he spotted a small tree from Queensland, *E. beaninna*, and in a thoughtful tone told her that not long ago he'd overheard an oldish woman on a Manly ferry comment to a woman who may have been her daughter, "That's a terrible name! It's going to be a millstone around her neck."

He turned to Ellen, "Ah-ha, she smiles."

Speaking of millstones, what about the technical sales manager of an industrial ceramics firm, Sydney again, who for some reason always ended up losing authority in the workplace?

He had the name Been – Peter Been.

Obviously whenever a person in a jovial tone enquired, "Been all right?" it seemed to be casting aspersions on this man, wherever he happened to be. Even the habit of his innocent salesmen to begin a message "has been today" pointed a finger at his declining abilities. In the rapidly changing, low-margin world of industrial ceramics the slightest suggestion of someone being a "has-been" is . . . unfortunately it's the kiss of death.

Ellen was still pondering the power of companionship, the story of the poor cobbler.

Really, puns are invariably a nuisance – and of no consequence. They're seen as a way to shift to one side of the true essence of things, an evasion which doesn't get anyone anywhere. At least they have made very little headway in the traditional method of naming trees, and that includes the eucalypts.

"Do you know my name?" she asked.

"Of course. But don't ask me now."

They had stopped before another eucalypt, a gaudy one, miraculously transplanted from Melville Island, its maroon flowers hovering on a green-brown sea, a shawl from Kashmir without the fancy borders. And as Ellen saw him thinking on his feet she leaned against the trunk, and waited.

"From now on, I won't mention a single pun. Nup," he put his hand on his heart, "nothing artificial."

* *

As they went from tree to tree and he told other stories, Ellen allowed them slowly to circle and enter her. Over time his voice vibrated along with the familiar heat, through the trees. She liked the sound of his voice. In the heat of the day she felt like closing her eyes. Instead she surveyed him, as she listened. She didn't even know his name. What if someone asked?

By the time Ellen had to return to the house this man had told her another six or seven – she didn't count them – stories.

20

Desertorum

Y ES YES YES yes: in Zurich, in Dublin, in a motor
mechanic's garage in Paris many a story begins and
ends with this most pleasing of words, still more pleasing
to the ear, if not to the mind's eye, than *eucalyptus*. And,
yes, every man in town, women also, mothers first and
foremost, had been coming out with "yes" to Holland
before he had opened his mouth – if not the actual word
it was in their expressions – anything to keep on the good
side of the canny possessor of all those rolling acres,
prime river-frontage going to waste, and his beautiful
daughter. She certainly was beautiful; and with each day
she was growing more beautiful, a speckled pigeon-egg
that far exceeded anything in the district. The more
travelled men, such as those who'd been to the war, as
well as almost every suitor, could not recall a more beautiful woman, not in the nearest large town, or over the
mountains, in Sydney. The new manager of the corrugated-
iron bank let it be known he had not seen a finer beauty
in the entire city of London, where he'd spent three weeks
after the war.

And the landscape, it too had a speckled beauty which
seeped in geologically from all directions, and remained.

Holland was satisfied with its steady appearance – its slow rise and fall, the wear and tear which showed as mere scratching of the surface. The trees, the trees. In all it had taken many years for Holland to accept the pale strength of the land. It had crept into his body, as it were, and settled, always there. He would forget all about it then – a gift, a natural advantage, which is to be envied.

Whereas Ellen's thoughts returned to Sydney, often to the school and her earnest friends, or to a nondescript street corner: manufactured foundations. There was always a sea wall and the heavy slop and glitter of the harbour, and the city streets, its shops and crowds of people heading in different directions. Often while standing in a paddock Ellen pictured herself somewhere else; and how could that ever happen? It was given form in her journal, and by the direction of her thoughts as they drifted from the tower and in the hot dirt among the trees, or when she herself drifted in the warm current of the river – a form of double-drift. Without harshness Ellen could separate herself from the property of trees and her father she loved.

Superimposed on landscape is art. And what a hectic, apparently essential endeavour it is!

Art is imperfect, unlike nature which is casually "perfect". To try to repeat or even convey by hand some corner of nature is forever doomed. And yet the strange power of art lies in our recognition of this attempt.

The artist, yes, humanises the wonder of nature by doing a faulty version of it; and so nature – landscape, the figure – is brought closer to us, putting it faintly within our grasp. See the human versions of water lilies, the mountain outside Aix, the yellow flat earth of the Wimmera; sunflowers, bathers too, not to mention the oak tree with dog running in from the right, which presumably represents all trees on earth. The brush marks, the insects stuck in the paint, thumb-prints, the *signature* and so on are signs of human effort. When these are not there, as in photography, the result remains parallel to nature, opportunistic.

Otherwise, a given landscape such as Holland's continues to cry out for conversion into human terms.

Both Holland and Mr Cave had little time for mirrors. If it were not for shaving they probably would not have one in the house, or anywhere else for that matter. For the same reason – if there's any poetic logic in the world – they were uncomfortable with the act of giving or receiving.

On the morning of the ninth day Mr Cave got around these difficult feelings by sliding a brown paper bag across the table, explanations thereby unnecessary. Holland acknowledged the gesture by over-ignoring it, taking his time to finish his cup of tea. Ellen almost felt sorry for them. Eventually, Holland got around to tilting the bag: out slid the definitive edition of a common subject, *Dust* by S. Cyril Blacktin (Chapman & Hall, 1934).

"It's my birthday," Mr Cave explained. "I'm feeling generous."

"Happy birthday," said Holland. He turned a few pages. "Where are the pictures?"

"Will you read it?" his daughter asked.

"Who knows?"

He'd add it to his shelf of anthographies and field guides, the stacks of *Illustrated London News* and *Walkabout*. There was a dog-eared copy of Kaleski's classic, *Australian Barkers and Biters*, and ledgers with suede spines he'd never opened.

Instead of putting everybody in a good mood the unexpected gift subdued them, Ellen too. It reminded them all that the contest was coming to an end.

Mr Cave saw it in different colours, which meant going over old ground.

"Shallow roots," Ellen heard him saying. "They haven't really taken in this place. And the soil, there's thinness in the soil. I'd say we haven't been here long enough, we don't go in deep. I often think about it. In my family there's failure. You know the type of thing: drunks, no-hopers among the men, a lot of that. My ancestors arrived, yes, and we've continued and grown, but that's about it. Nothing more than that . . . "

"I wouldn't lose any sleep over it, if I were you," said Holland.

As soon as they were out of sight Ellen decided to "lose herself", if that was ever possible, not in the rectilinear formations along the river, but among the clusters of dishevelled mallees below the homestead, past the wind-break. On pleasant whim she wore the pale red shoes with high-ish heels she'd bought in Sydney. These were designed for traversing short distances of carpet, little more. Ellen had worn them only in her bedroom. Now on the cracked earth between the trees Ellen skirted a vast ants' nest, and lurching a little enjoyed holding her elbows out in an exaggerated manner as the tapering heels kept spearing into the clutter of barks. The impracticality of the little shoes actually pleased her: it drew her own thoughts down to her ankles, from where they somehow represented her feelings in general – of being both free and spectacularly vulnerable.

She was still allowing her body to sway and angle, because she could imagine herself, when she saw him.

"You've been watching," she protested.

Taking off the shoes she put them under her arm.

"Haven't you?"

"Put them on again," he said. He was frowning at the shoes.

But she would be exposed in front of him; and he would reach out to steady her, with his eyes at least. She wondered why he was there. He was nothing like a suitor, not really. Wherever she went he appeared, near a tree.

He must have been watching her.

He shook his head. "Not necessarily," he said.

"Are you all right?" she asked. He was pale.

Any one of the suitors first vetted by her father would have by then blurted out with a tight face the name of the tree he now squatted under, a Hooked Mallee (*E. desertorum*).

He didn't say anything for a while.

"I've a suggestion." He smoothed a space at arm's length. "Take the weight off your feet."

Looking down, Ellen could see a portion of his neck.

"But I don't mind if you keep standing. What I can tell you is this . . . it's a bare statement I once heard. At least put your shoes down, or give them to me! In Lebanon, on the fringe of the desert is a place called Valley-of-Saints. Here, it is said, lived three holy men who practised miracles.

"Ah, she's sitting down. That's good.

"One holy man could cure things like rheumatism; one, they claim, could raise a dead person to life; and the third one, the one we are concerned with here, had given children many times to barren wives. He had more visits than the other two put together.

"Deserts," he went on, as if he'd spent a lot of time wandering across them, "are places of unearthly *cleanliness*. They say it produces clarity in a person."

If he had wandered in faraway places and was now here, Ellen believed she would like him more. The way he behaved, what he said, and even his appearance interested her; and yet she was uncertain. As always he was both near and far. He assumed she would be interested in his stories. Several times as she glanced at him she caught him looking away.

He continued the story. "A woman made the long journey across the desert to visit the holy man. More than anything else she wanted a child, but she had been unable to have a child. She was poor. To save leather she walked barefoot, carrying her shoes. And on her return, within a year, she had a son. But then as she made the long journey barefoot back to the holy man, carrying her baby for him to baptise, the child died. In the desert she became aware of its limbs growing cold in her arms. That was in Lebanon."

In the silence Ellen was assaulted with the desert panorama, the single shawled figure reduced to shuffling, and questions going begging. She turned to him. And there he was. Leaning back with both elbows on the ground and knees raised, gazing across at another tree.

"Where did you hear that?"

"It's a desert story. I think there are many like it. It must be an old story."

Before she could ask, "Why tell it to me?" he'd narrowed his eyes like Major Lawrence in the film. "Unless I'm mistaken, correct me if I'm wrong . . . isn't that what's called a Boranup Mallee?"

And while Ellen still saw the poor woman with the empty arms the stranger (who was no longer a complete stranger), after a pause for thought, took from the slender tree with the pinkish-grey trunk another story, in another desert. On the dirt road south of Darwin, he said, there is a motel café with Shell petrol pumps. It was hot, and I can still see the strange tension between the Latvian who ran the place, and the plump woman who served meals, including breakfast, for the passing travellers. She wore a scarf knotted at the top of her head. He had small eyes, a smooth forehead, and short hair. First thing in the morning the Latvian opened a bottle of beer, and drank during the day. Outside was a huge mountain of bottles. I noticed busloads of tourists lining up to photograph it. There were chooks and some goats on long chains. There was also a White Russian, who lived in a caravan out the back fitted with an air conditioner.

He looked at Ellen and appeared to nod significantly.

The White Russian was actually the husband of the woman, but had been displaced by the Latvian, a younger man, who'd allowed the husband to stay in the caravan, where I was told he spent his spare time painting snow scenes on emu eggs. Did I say she was plump, good-natured, untidy? The White Russian was willing to work for nothing in the garage, just to be near his wife. He was careful with the Latvian only to protect her, still his wife. Some mornings she appeared with her face swollen and bruised. I can tell you the husband's name: Turczaninov.

This small settlement of two men and a woman was in the middle of nowhere and surrounded in all directions by red earth. Their water came from a bore, sunk a hundred years ago, lined with ironbark. One morning in February the Latvian complained of a splitting headache. By evening he had some sort of fever. The next day he could no longer speak. He was thrashing about on his bed. He sweated buckets. He was muttering words not even the woman, another Latvian, knew.

The woman no longer served customers food as she tried putting ice on the sick man's forehead, and the White Russian remained in his caravan, not bothering to serve petrol, or replace the broken windscreens on the cars of passing travellers. On the third day the man went very quiet. The woman left his bed and hammered on the door of the caravan. After a while the White Russian came out and followed his wife into what had once been their bedroom. Telling her not to worry he lifted the man from his sick-bed and with a set expression that could only have come from the steppes carried him out to the bore.

Gently he placed him in the metal bucket, and made him secure with ropes. Then he lowered the sick man far down, to the end of the line, drenching him in the cold water. Three times he did it.

The sick man opened his eyes, and as he slowly came up he passed through his life, the evenly spaced horizontal slabs of ironbark as regular as the months and years. He saw his parents seated at the metal table under a tree in Riga; snow and lights at night; going back through paths with other children to see the dead soldier in the forest for over a year as it decomposed, without ever telling anyone; he passed his sister's mouth who spoke slowly otherwise she'd get "dizzy"; thin schoolteacher blind in one eye; aunt's teeth and pale swaying breasts; "Shut up!"; the rusted hinge on the front gate; after the three broken ribs he noticed more wax in one ear; wanted to grasp the passing geometry of a fern's leaf; pissed himself; took huge bite out of an apple and another; smooth-skinned young woman turned into the lines of his mother; sudden complete disappearance of their father; he passed the nothing between his sister's legs; the way he looked up to older men; blackheads on that policeman's nose; mother again, loose dress; during war, afternoons suddenly smelt like a butcher's shop; a woman's contempt; dirty ankles of the girl; uniforms and general overall dullness; streets of mud; passing huge gaps in his life, huge gaps; ferns, wet earth, large black birds; I've got to laugh; roaring water; she's opening her thighs; the look on Turczaninov's face the day he jailed Turczaninov for twenty years and how the very same day he went and helped himself to the man's wife; the idea in silhouette of New York; he can't get close enough, he could never get close enough; took the rifle the first week in Australia and shot the eagle – hit the ground with a thump; lack of any idea in his head but he didn't mind; thirsty; two trees against a sky; a given life consists of the right amount of time, he saw; a glass filling to the top with water; it passes slowly; white light. These were the sorts of things he would have seen. The point was he reached the surface in the desert south of Darwin, the White Russian Turczaninov lifted him gently under the dripping shoulders, and he was dead.

21

Cameronii

I T WAS NECESSARY to pass through patches of masculine behaviour. Accounts of physical courage were always difficult to ignore.

A military trench threw a deep shadow across his mind, ready and waiting for his use. Each scenario was an all-too-easily imagined situation, activating in slow motion a rehearsal of his own possible behaviour. A matter of remaining quick and calm at the same time, often in mud. No sign of a woman anywhere, no fluttering of the soft cotton dress.

These postmortems on violence could easily turn into stories of importance. Even reduced to fragments, the way a rifle is dismantled, there is always the possibility of them tipping over into the depths of myth, a very deep echo effect.

Stories dressed in khaki had little interest for Ellen – just as in Sydney she'd barely glanced at the frigates and cruisers moored at Woolloomooloo. Now as he worked his way through the quota of them she sat cross-legged and, appearing to listen good-naturedly – though she was only demonstrating tolerance – bent her neck like a pale swan to examine her bare sole.

God knows, there is enough in the names of eucalypts to trigger quite a riveting recollection concerning war, and other examples of extreme (that is to say, normal) masculine behaviour.

There are at least forty species of eucalypts known as boxes: Fuzzy Box, Craven Grey Box, Molloy Box, and so on. In producing stories for Ellen the stranger sidestepped as too ordinary the possible connection between them and, say, the one about the abysmal Aboriginal southpaw with the tattooed bottle-blonde combing her hair in his corner, or Molloy, the Great White Hope from Lithgow, who retired from the ring without a mark on his face – even had all his own teeth – and became a prosperous tractor and used-car dealer in a country town, to then suffer a personal tragedy with his only son. Stories gather pace inside the ring, and spread to the outside.

As for the Spotted Gum (*E. maculata*), it is immediately apparent the mottled khaki-green trunk is a replica of the camouflage worn by the Australian army. It allowed the stranger to preface some stories with the observation that on the best authority, beginning with Captain Graves of the Royal Welch Fusiliers, Australian troops had the worst reputations for violence against prisoners – *worse than the Moroccans and the Turks*. The reason might be that, beginning in the Great War, large numbers of volunteers came from the rural districts, where slaughter is a part of the working week. There was one countryman who managed to avoid both wars, he recalled (Ellen wasn't concentrating), and on the river property he shared with his brothers he built the most melancholy memorial to the dead, a private bridge for the exclusive use of sheep.

Another obvious candidate for story-prompting was the bloodwoods, recognisable by their haemorrhage of red sap; Holland had a stand of about thirty, down the southern end. Mention *blood* to a given man and infantry battles, car crashes, cut fingers come to mind, whereas for Ellen blood had a flowing, altogether more central meaning. There is a lean old soldier in Canberra with an incredible red face. As a young officer he had leapt into trenches in North Africa and New Guinea, and taken on the enemy single-handed. Bloodwood. On more than one occasion his rifle butt and he himself were splashed all over in blood. He had several wounds and medals to show for it. In civilian life, it was he who composed the printed citations accompanying awards for conspicuous bravery, a voluntary task he succeeded in completely monopolising. Over the years he developed a mastery of laconic description, which could withstand endless repetition: "under extreme . . . ", "although heavily outnumbered . . . ", "with disregard for his own personal safety . . .", "returning under heavy fire . . . ", etc. And yet, like so many other physically courageous men, at home he was in constant retreat from his wife and four daughters, and found it easier to be out of the house when it came to matters of subtlety and principle; what might be called a jovial and popular "moral coward".

They passed through the last of the bloodwoods. It was hot. As Ellen followed, she vaguely saw him as some sort of wandering warrior. That's a good one – in amongst the gum trees, a *wandering warrior*. Isn't that out of a heavy old volume fitted with a prohibitive brass lock?

Sometimes Ellen concentrated on a figure leaning against a shell-blasted tree, covered in dust, weary from loss of blood; he could even be on horseback . . .

She still didn't know his name. For a moment Ellen thought of asking her father if he knew him.

For that matter, why couldn't Mr Cave be a warrior from distant parts? Under the eye of her unforgiving father he displayed a matter-of-fact calm, not a hair out of place. And there was a soldierly aspect in his complexion and bearing; his safari suit was distinctly paramilitary; so Ellen constructed, through half-closed eyes.

At the mouth of a gully spilling orange boulders was a tall and lanky tree, *E. exserta*.

Strolling past it he pondered its common name, "Messmate". In the last war, he said, two Australian soldiers met on the troopship to the Middle East, and had a loud argument about racehorses. From that day they were seen as mates. The short one was hoping to be a dentist in Brisbane, his mate worked for a brewery. The easy depth of their friendship was noticeable when, after eating in the mess, they would go on talking and be the last to leave. There was no awkwardness. With them it wasn't necessary to be always saying something. Although they didn't really know much about each other, and didn't ask, not wanting to get personal, they would go out of their way to help one another. Fruitcakes shipped from home in soldered tins, cigarettes and toothbrushes were just some of the things they shared. A street photographer in Jerusalem has them pulling faces in front of the canvas backdrop of a paltry oasis, one wearing a fez and the Queensland grin, draping an arm over the other's shoulder.

149

Every few days the short one wrote to a girl in Brisbane he was engaged to marry. Holding her photograph at arm's length his friend gave a low whistle, although even he must have noticed her prominent teeth.

The short one, the possible dentist, was earnest and almost pedantic, especially when recalling his fiancée waiting for him back home, while the one who let out the whistle was lanky, loud and easy-going, and passed easily through the world. He was called Brain which prevented him, as he said, from ever becoming an officer.

It wasn't long afterwards, in the battle for Crete, the short one lost his right eye and hand from a grenade. Alongside him, his lanky friend, Brain, caught some shrapnel in the stomach.

Both were evacuated. In the military hospital they had adjoining beds, and the tall one began making a good recovery.

Needless to say, the severely wounded one, who was almost entirely obscured by bandages, and without an eye and a hand, was in no condition to write to his fiancée, let alone on a regular basis. Even when his friend placed a cigarette to his lips he had trouble inhaling.

Brain who was back on his feet took it upon himself to write to the fiancée. Without thinking, he didn't bother introducing himself, using instead the familiar "I".

In Brisbane, the young woman suddenly began receiving letters from a soldier with completely unfamiliar handwriting. After some hesitation, she replied.

She thanked him for his letters. She asked if by chance he knew her fiancé, a short man with ginger hair. Several times she asked. Aided by the irregularities of war – ships were being sunk every day in the Mediterranean – presumably containing his letters – he gave no answer. Instinct told him not to describe his friend's terrible injuries. Instead he redoubled his efforts at amusing her. Gradually she began asking him about himself.

In that hospital with green walls the hours passed slowly. He'd seen war; and that was it. All he wanted to do now was return home. He told her of his plans to buy a country pub. He'd gone into it. Country pubs were surprisingly cheap. He sketched out a gentle life in tune with the seasons and the flow of shearers and commercial travellers. His letters were now running to a dozen or more pages. The young woman's teeth so prominent in all their innocence receded, and he pictured only her good-natured squint and, from his memory of the torn photograph, the flow of her hips.

Meanwhile, the would-be dentist remained on the danger list, and Brain, who gave false symptoms to the doctors to be near his friend, wheeled him out into the sunlight and sat alongside him in a cane chair and wrote the letters. On one of these brief journeys his friend groaned when he was bumped. Another time he felt for his friend's arm, "You're the best."

Gradually, almost accidentally, the letters became brazen, highly suggestive. From his memory of the photograph he extravagantly praised her hips, and her feet, which were not even in the photograph, and offered speculations on her personality. In slow detail he stripped her of clothes, described her underwear, until she stood entirely naked before him, so he wrote. He was a soldier, and a soldier is expected to be brave.

151

Cautiously she responded. She made a light joke. But did he seriously imagine she would be offended?

No longer was his handwriting unfamiliar to her. The firm flow and the dark ink had an insistence page after page which matched the words, the thoughts he couldn't avoid expressing. And since he was now writing every day she would scarcely recover from one set of long-distant daydreams, which read as persistent demands, before another would arrive, followed by another; or, because of the irregularities of war, a batch of seven or eight. To use a recent military term: a version of carpet bombing, difficult to survive.

Slowly the badly wounded one recovered enough to be shipped home, although his eyesight was poor. Walking alongside as they carried him onto the ship his friend said he'd look him up at the end of the war. They shook hands and exchanged addresses.

At that moment – the worst possible moment – a crow began its desolate lament. Before Ellen could say anything the story-teller turned.

"You could always begin," he smiled at her, "by looking in at the country hotels here and there, those with the deep verandahs. Examine the teeth of every fifty-plus woman serving behind the bar."

Again this stranger on her property was leading the way; Ellen was conscious of following him – she could be somewhere else, doing other things.

They were a long way from the house.

Strolling on he didn't appear interested in her; often he didn't even bother to wave at the flies. And yet they had drifted about for hours together, without apparent self-consciousness, the way strangers sit comfortably together in a darkened picture theatre.

"Shouldn't you be getting back?" he suddenly asked. "What's the time?"

It was a question that didn't require an answer; often these remain suspended as the most pleasant, open statements. What would she say if her father asked where she had been? Words and words, hour after hour, from tree to tree.

The way he was drawn towards one tree and not another was like a length of lead wire forming a triangle, pulling him in along a straight line. As Ellen entered the stories, or his sketches for stories, she saw how they grew from the names of the eucalypts, usually the less fancy common names. And if many of the stories were based on the flimsiest foundations, or even a complete misreading of a name, it hardly mattered.

Here out in the open was an *E. cameronii*, fairly tall, with grey fibrous bark.

He pulled off a strip of its soft bark, which produced a cloud of dust.

They remained within the frail shade of the *cameronii*, which actually resembled a photographic negative of foliage, and the way he began moving in and out of the shade suggested he had realised a story, another one from his dwindling stock of war stories, stories of violence, which are grey-dark stories. And Ellen was not yet sure grey was a colour she liked, whether for a ship, a pair of shoes, a dress – masculine, metallic. There were a few exceptions, of course, such as certain winter skies and the soft feathers of the galah which bleed so harmoniously into pink.

Stories she felt drawn to were not grey stories with slabs of black, but those that involved the green, red and strong blue gusts and geometrical switches among three people, so deep and shocking she simply had to scribble them down in her journal.

With her fingertips Ellen touched the beauty spots distributed over her cheeks.

"Small town in the Republic of Ireland," he began, "by the name of Lifford."

Such a genial, abbreviated beginning avoided other fruitful possibilities: "It was a rainy night in Boston," for example; or, "Strange sensation then (August 26)," not to mention "The Marquis left at five." Still, in his favour, he had made a harmless exaggeration: Lifford is really a village, not a town. Slate roofs, wet streets, unusually erratic schoolchildren.

"Lifford, as one glance on the map will tell, is like unhappy towns in Poland and Czechoslovakia. It has the misfortune to straddle the border between two countries . . ."

In Lifford, some houses had their front lounge room in Northern Ireland, and the bathroom and back garden in the Republic. An invisible dotted line ran through the town and people's lives. Aside from anything else it aggravated savage loyalties. A young man called Kearney had grown up in Lifford, one of five Catholic children. He was very clear on what he wanted to do. Like many of the young men he wanted to leave Lifford. But even Dublin to the south seemed on the other side of the world. Although he was out of work he began saving for a motorbike. Kearney was a drinker. To take out the Protestant girls from the nearby farms he crossed the border at night. He kissed them behind trees and stone walls. A great one for cracking jokes. He had a big mouth. At night in the fields and lanes he saw men he recognised, as well as strangers with weapons and cars without lights; he saw a dead British soldier in a culvert, and a Protestant still twitching, wearing a cloth cap.

Some older men suggested he think about keeping his mouth shut, and that he leave the farm girls alone. If he was warned he took no notice. He was told again.

Kearney was returning to Lifford one night from seeing a girl back to her house. This girl who lived in Northern Ireland had allowed him to undo the front of her blouse. As Kearney crossed back into the Republic he was whistling, both hands in his pockets.

A man lighting a cigarette stepped out in front of him. Others came forward. Kearney looked around and tried to bluff. In daylight or inside a bar he could have charmed them. A fist or an axe-handle struck the side of his head with terrific force. It seemed to break his head open. There was another blow in his face, then others, still more from other sides. He felt his nose go. To gain sympathy he fell to the ground, and curled up, where it was worse, for it attracted their boots. So many parts of him were cracking, splitting. He felt himself going. He was only dimly aware why. He remembered feeling relieved: there's no pain. He also wondered about his motorbike. Less than an hour ago these hard teeth had touched the pale breast of the solemn farm girl, and now Kearney cried out as they snapped and bits of them fell inside his mouth.

In the struggle one side of his body was beaten up in Northern Ireland, the other in the Republic. His ribs broken and lungs punctured on one side, the fractured cheekbone, fingers and ankle on the other.

One side of his body was beaten black, the other blue. One eye closed.

Kearney was left half-dead, half-alive. Not even he was sure. Early in the morning he was found by the milkman lying in a puddle, more dead than alive.

It was as if – from that day on – one part of his feelings was dead, the other alive. It was pleasant talking to Kearney, for a while. He didn't express an opinion, he didn't take sides. One part of him would think one thing, the other part the opposite. On the one hand this, on the other hand that.

With a disability pension he moved to Dublin. There he drifted into photography.

For a person who adopted a neutral position on any given situation a career in photography was ideal, and after easily handling an apprenticeship as a police photographer, his extreme qualities of dispassionate even-handedness were recognised by Fleet Street, and Kearney was given the difficult assignments of civil wars and famines and executions in Africa and South America, assignments which had wrecked the peace of mind of others before him. Kearney showed no feelings about what he saw. His black-and-white photographs became famous in the Sunday magazines for their harsh objectivity.

And in those busy years Kearney himself became a

familiar figure with his battered face, crooked leg and permanent camera bag.

In one of the newspaper offices in London he met an Australian journalist from a country newspaper in New South Wales. She had strident views on everything under the sun. Perhaps he saw something of his old self in her! Besides, she found his extreme ability to see both sides attractive. He tended to balance her; at the same time, she could see she'd be able to manage him – a life of some consistency.

No sooner had they married than she suggested they move to Sydney. One city was the same as any other city, as far as he was concerned, although in Sydney it meant beginning all over again with his camera doing police work.

It was she who convinced him to avoid black-and-white photography, and turn to colour. That was all right by him. Colour could achieve things that black-and-white couldn't, and vice versa. From a terrace house in Newtown, where doors and windows open and gasp in the humidity – gritty suburb, Newtown – they started a small business producing photographic calendars for stock agents, greengrocers and butchers to hand out in December, every year featuring a photograph of a paddock full of merinos, or a view of the same solitary Ghost Gum from different angles.

The business has not prospered. Nor has it declined.

To get an opinion out of Kearney is still impossible. He never argues. She has begun going to church. They appear to be a contented couple.

22

Rudis

THE IDEA THAT a tranquil man would have a violent imagination doesn't seem possible; and yet signs of the Napoleonic phenomenon are quite common in the outer reaches of Protestantism. In fact, it may not be at all far-fetched to claim that tranquillity and violent imagination are precisely what have attracted men to serve in the church in the first place. So common is this trait among ministers, pastors and missionaries it can be ignored by the Protestant leaders at their own peril. In certain conservative parishes, or when a seemingly tranquil man is shipped out to a strange and difficult country as a missionary, there's always the possibility of unseemly conduct. Missionary work, incidentally, appears to be at odds with the cardinal rule, "In seatedness and quietness the soul acquires wisdom."

The story of Clarence Brown – the Reverend Clarence Brown – begins, for our purposes, not in Edinburgh where he was born, but on a river in 1903 in West Africa, in his early thirties, and finishes up (more or less) in suburban Adelaide and other parts of Australia, his traces scattered.

His father was a preacher in Edinburgh who loved the ocean-rolling surge of his own voice. Even "good morning" on the steps of the church was spoken with such conviction that veins bulged in his temples and forehead. It came as little surprise to the congregation one Sunday when he seemed to stammer, with his arm raised as if holding up a broad sword, and pitched forward in the pulpit.

Clarence knelt beside his father. "Go ye . . . " he seemed to be trying to say, before letting out a final sigh from the deep. Clarence had decided anyway. In early 1903 he landed in Lagos with his young wife, and the following day travelled up the River Niger to a remote hot village.

Nothing had prepared the Reverend Brown and his bonneted wife for Africa's incredible heat, the signs of illness and starvation, and everywhere an air of impassive hopelessness. He had been to London once, that was all.

The bewildering strangeness of the country was made more melancholy by the breadth of the river and the distance between people and objects. From the moment they landed in Africa and the further they went up river they felt forgotten by their own people, another tribe decked out in elaborate clothes and customs. Rubbing his hands the Reverend did his best to console his wife who was missing the piano and her many sisters in Edinburgh. In the heat she had gone red in the face and breathed through her mouth. She hated the slightest noise outside and refused to handle babies.

No rain had fallen in that part of the world for seven years.

The crops had withered away, affecting the eyesight and bones of second-born children, and the communal wealth which consisted of untidy herds of black-and-white goats was decimated, permanently altering the dowry system. For the first time in living memory the River Niger had stopped flowing, and from upstream came reports of it flowing *backwards*. To the people who grew up along its banks, the world as they knew it was coming to an end.

If the entire shape of the river was simple and visible, like the sun or the moon, or a tree, or even fire, it might have been worshipped. The people took their river seriously. It passed by their lives, always there, and gave life to others. There were stories, again from upstream, of bodies floating down in flood and stopping outside houses to point to a faithless wife.

Normally the river's strength could be felt with a hand. Now that it had stopped flowing and was nothing more than a long warm pond a similar lassitude entered the people, which caused the Reverend Brown to weaken, then rapidly to lose all appearance of tranquillity.

He was like something out of the Old Testament. The gaunt figure stumbling around in a barren landscape is cannon fodder for the fables. He was a good man; it showed in a kind of hectic innocence. He could not bear to see people suffer – the children, the children. As a new arrival and a white man invested with religious powers he became the point of focus. He had to do something.

They kept looking at him, singly, in groups.

Wearing his full religious regalia the Reverend Brown prayed for rain, first in private, then alongside his silent wife – who had become unaccountably savage to the natives; then in the sweltering corrugated-iron church; and, when that failed, by the river itself before a large crowd. He looked up into the heavens: hot, entirely cloudless. This went on for weeks. He heard his own words rolling out as thunder; someone was in full control of misery and death – he called out if anyone was listening; until in a rhythmic momentum of hope and bewilderment, perhaps inherited from his father, he rushed from the church and threw into the river the large wooden statue of Christ.

Later the same day the great river seemed to move. The following day it was flowing strongly. Within a week nothing was stopping it: the river broadened, broke its banks. Frail animals and the few crops were carried away; old people and children weakened by famine too; makeshift huts along the banks swept away; even Brown's church, which was supposed to occupy the higher ground, was flooded.

To these story-telling people the Reverend had brought nothing but trouble. Since his arrival their miseries had multiplied. Behind his back was a flood of abuse. Brown couldn't understand why his weekly sermons were ignored. Reports reached London of his difficulties and the shocking action of throwing Christ into the water – aside from anything else, the statue was church property – and he was recalled, never to set foot again in Africa.

In Adelaide, which is the city of eucalypts, Clarence Brown and his wife settled in a bungalow with a red verandah in the suburb of Norwood. The placid suburb of faded grey paling fences produced a calming effect, at least in her. With his surplus of energies he became busy as a lay preacher and a furniture removalist during the week.

They had a daughter. At eighteen she was forced to marry an older man. For a while her father tried to keep her condition hidden inside the house; but when that was no longer possible he sent her, against her mother's pleadings, away.

The man she married was an insurance executive, always on the road. His name was Cave. Their child born was a son, who grew up strong and close to his mother. Due to the circumstances she became extremely dependent on him. Avoiding church she took him instead to concerts, always in the same two seats. And he never failed to be concerned at how music encouraged a violent imagination in his mother, parting her mouth, ruffling the normal tranquillity of her face, sometimes producing a tear. He still sat with her in concerts; but Mr Cave remained wary of music, which is written to the glory of God.

For a while he tried standing back to picture himself. Although solid in his socks he saw himself as a light and sketchy presence. Very easily did Mr Cave feel accidental.

At least the world of trees offered a solid base. After all, here was an entire world, psychology-free, a world both open and closed. The task of classification and description was complexity enough. Eucalypts, for example, were an intricate subject he could almost contain with his own shape, as if it was a single, endlessly reproducing person.

More than once Mr Cave had been on the point of telling Holland some of this – as if the telling would make any difference; but he decided instead it was Ellen who would show more sympathy. It was about time he opened up a conversation with her.

It was simpler with Holland to meander in and out of the subject of eucalypts. Exchange of information was easy – easier – for both of them. Mr Cave could do this as he went on naming the trees. On his many field trips along the Murray and the Darling, and Cooper Creek and beyond, Mr Cave heard stories about floods, almost as many as about bushfires or inexperienced people getting lost and dying of thirst. Walking with Holland across his property Mr Cave felt compelled to tell some of these stories, and Holland mentioned one in passing to Ellen, because it included a woman in town they both knew.

Not so many years ago during the shortage of school-teachers, the story went, the government advertised in Great Britain. A science teacher with a pale wife and two daughters arrived and was sent to Grafton – one of those northern river towns.

They moved into a wooden house, not far from the river. They'd hardly got used to this vast land, let alone the ways of the small country town, Grafton – they'd been there barely a week – when the river rose and overflowed its banks. Still more water came down – brown, unstoppable, and everywhere. The teacher and his family were taken from their house by boat.

After the flood there was mud. It stained the walls. The teacher had to use his shoulder to open the door to the bedroom, and when it opened his wife and daughters shrieked and stepped back. The flood had deposited in their bedroom a dead cow, where it lay rotting and bloated on the double bed.

What a country! It was enough to make anyone catch the first boat back to the postcard greenery of England.

But they stayed on. He became a headmaster.

And their daughters, they eventually married in country towns. One of them is the gasbag at the post office, Holland told Ellen; the one with the brown hair set like headphones. Traces of a Midlands accent remain, the way a flood deposits a trail above a window.

From the day Ellen stepped off the train this woman in town had followed her progress. The child was without a mother! Often she asked Ellen questions about her father, at least early on. Noting the suitors who made their way out to the property the postmistress found herself almost every day handing a letter to Mr Cave, or selling him a maroon stamp. Although he was somewhat older than Ellen, she fancied his chances; he was a solid, dependable type.

23

Racemosa

A FINE EXAMPLE of the Flooded Gum (*E. rudis*) can be seen at the Botanic Gardens in Sydney, thirty paces back from the bookshop. It certainly has a towering grandeur. *Magnificent* comes to mind. Of course it does. *Magnificent* is to be avoided at all costs, above all in describing a work of art, such as a Cézanne (the painter of pines), or the vulgarities of an opera house, or even the physique of a brown boxer ("magnificent specimen"), let alone the natural majesty of a gum tree. It really is a puffed-up term, a sign of impotence in the person poised with the pen, striving to convey . . . better for all concerned if it was returned for use alongside *magnify*, and left at that.

In girth and habitat the Flooded Gum is similar to the River Red Gum, preferring watercourses and swampy ground; and yet it has been successfully cultivated in sandy Algeria. *Rudis* apparently refers to the rough bark; either that or its timber – good for nothing but firewood.

Its upper branches are smooth and grey. Buds are larger with a bluntly conic operculum; adult leaves are petiolate.

Holland's example was at right angles to the bridge, and

next in line stood a pale Scribbly Gum, this one called *E. racemosa*.

So absorbed had Ellen become in the slowly told stories of the stranger, so much a part of her day now, she took little notice of the eucalypts behind the stories; she allowed the world, which was his and far beyond, to come to her. His roundabout way of telling one story after another depended on imagination and a breadth of experience, and meant he was spending hours with her and her alone, revealing a little of himself at a time – only to disappear whenever he felt like it, sometimes with just a brief wave. To be then left surrounded by nothing but grey trunks, and a near-absence of anything stirring, added a scratchy, unsatisfied quality to the silence.

Eucalypts are notorious for giving off an inhospitable, unsympathetic air.

On this Friday morning she put on a dress faded to butter colour and felt loose and free; so much so she ruffled her beauty with a look of determined impatience. And she felt so aware of her own self within the sleeveless dress she flowed forward in a kind of bonelessness, so it felt.

Out in the open there was precious little focus. At least the stranger could be relied upon to make one of his appearances; he was a shape to anticipate, separate from the trees.

The voice was familiar – searching, faint gravel. If he read to her, she would fall asleep.

This time he was unexpectedly personal.

"They're interesting," he eyed her below the throat, "they suit you very well."

They were large white buttons below the V, only two. She'd taken them from an old coat and sewn them on herself.

"My father went that way," she said, "so I came this way. I feel I'm deceiving him."

"I don't see why." Frowning, he gave the cable of the rickety bridge a firm rattle.

Ellen was aware she had stepped away from what he originally said, leaving before him nothing but fresh air, when he had actually shown an interest in her. She turned to the formation of evenly spaced trunks between them and the house.

"It's my favourite lot of trees. What is yours?" Before he could answer she said softly, "Have you been in there? I saw once a photo of a rubber plantation in Malaya . . ."

He held a finger up. Eagles floating down from the great Mountain Ash veered away, and other dark birds joined the sky.

Now Ellen heard too: men's voices, boots crunching on strips of bark.

He pulled her into a space under the bridge, where they squatted, still holding her wrist, which she allowed.

She felt the smile in his voice, "Now you really are deceiving your father. What if he finds you here now?"

"Shhhh," she said.

Through a gap in the floor of the bridge she watched her father and Mr Cave coming into view, disappearing, reappearing, voices rising and falling too.

Ellen had been taking little notice of Mr Cave's progress; somehow she managed to put it at the back of her mind.

But now seeing it at close quarters she was shocked. As she watched he moved steadily through the trees and named the entire plantation in about forty minutes. Evidently her father had become resigned. As Mr Cave identified a tree he ticked it off like a tally clerk in some sort of home-made *catalogue raisonné*, with a black cover. Already they resembled a father trudging with son-in-law.

"He's like a machine," she said faintly.

She wanted to rest her head. It was the hopelessness – almost a spreading stain – she had forgotten about; it now filled her throat again, churning her stomach. She didn't know what to do. She went limp the way a woman is said to go limp on the verge of rape. Yet Mr Cave was not at all a bad man! Squashed under the bridge she became aware her wrist was still being held, a severe way of taking her pulse. At least he, this man, seemed to be neutral.

"This is terrible . . ." was all she could say.

The stranger let go of her wrist, and looked at the two men standing on the river bank to the right. It allowed Ellen to study the side of his face, his ear, and neck all very close.

"My father," Ellen whispered more to herself, "in the old coat. My father has . . ." Everybody for miles around knew about her father's marriage arrangement, though this man beside her had shown no sign of it.

At that stage Mr Cave had named over three-quarters of all the eucalypts; there could be only a few more days left. Fewer than a hundred trees remained, if that. Everybody else had fallen by the wayside. If Mr Cave wanted to he could have gone on and finished that very afternoon, except he seemed to enjoy walking around the paddocks with her father, talking and exchanging information, and not always about trees. Ellen saw all this before her; and now her father had become subdued.

To think that another man existed who also knew all there was to know about this vast and complex subject.

And Ellen suddenly wanted to march straight up and scream at her father, as if that would help. If only she was in Sydney. There she could disappear.

Just then his cigarette smoke reached them under the bridge. It contained the essence of him, her father; crumpled, warm, a stubborn presence, even to the silver furrows ploughed in his hair.

As for the stranger, he could hardly be relied upon. He took an interest, then appeared not to. He drew attention to the squat tree facing them, *E. racemosa*.

"Something's bound to turn up," he said.

Meanwhile, a prosaic photographer of trees (as other photographers aim for the nude, third-world walls, waifs in the melodramatic darkened drawing rooms, the aesthetics of famine and/or war, high fashion, mountains from various angles) on assignment for an international publisher had passed through Holland's property, after gaining his permission, and in a highly efficient process which had all the oblivious casualness of nature itself, had identified each and every eucalypt and taken a photograph of each of them. Working to a deadline it had taken several weeks. Wherever he happened to be setting up his camera the others were on the opposite side of the property. Then lugging his tripod like a theodolite he simply loaded up and drove out the front gate, not having a clue about the prize – there for the taking if only he knew about it – or if he had known was not interested, and was never seen again. Not even Ellen who had taken an instant dislike to his dark knotted beard and the boots and the khaki shorts knew what he had achieved.

24

Barberi

AT BREAKFAST HOLLAND sat in his rough coat prepared once more to step out.

Through the window: eucalypts here and there down to the flat alongside the river, its course marked by a greater congestion of green. To the left was part of the ornamental drive of evenly spaced, same-height eucalypts; remember how it went from the road to the front door.

It was late. Within easy reach of the prize Mr Cave could afford to take his time.

Clouds had filled the sky and pressed down over the land, a promise of longed-for rain. As a consequence, the air and parts of the earth were grey. The mood at the table was sombre, shadowy. It was probably exaggerated – aggravated, we can say – by the charcoal-grey brick of the house and the extra darkness cast by the deep verandahs.

Ellen felt grey. She hadn't slept.

She wondered if it was her own tiredness which made her father just then look . . . not exactly elderly, decidedly worn and settled. His ears had grown larger. And bits of his chin missed while shaving suggested somehow a lack of judgment in all other things.

"I want you to drink that. Otherwise I'm not pouring the tea."

At breakfast Ellen had been producing orange juice, if not for a longer life, to make him feel better.

Her father reached out for the glass. "In the opinion of Mr Cave, it was an act of madness and ignorance to plant eucalypts along the drive. He knows of at least three properties where it led a passing bushfire straight up to the house. And the whole lot went up in smoke. It could happen here, he said. What would we do then?"

He reached out and touched Ellen's elbow.

"The first thing our friend, Mr Cave, would do would be take the chainsaw to them. But nothing inside this house is of much value, except you. And without you" – he held her lovely elbow – "this here place would be an empty shell."

As Ellen remained beside him they became silent. She watched as he fiddled with his empty cup. He may have been on the point of saying something more when he looked up, "Hello, here is the man himself. Look at him, in his own way he's a remarkable chap."

Ellen hurriedly left the room. She didn't answer when her father called out, and again when he set out with Mr Cave. For a while her blue pillow became a comfort.

She glanced at herself in the mirror: all she was doing these days was frown. With a hurried carelessness she changed into an old shirt of her father's, boots and olive trousers. Outside, she strode as usual towards the river, but abruptly slowed, hardly walking at all, looking down at the ground. A lazy greyness stole over her.

She felt like a neat house about to be occupied. And she actually laughed.

Long past the suspension bridge Ellen found herself in a semi-enclosed area she had visited only once, many years before, with her father on one of his planting expeditions. This was the far northern end where the river took an eastern turn; at its furthermost point Holland had planted the solitary Ghost Gum, which could some days be seen from the town. To Ellen's right the hill sloped down towards the river, both in perpetual shadow. Here on the tapering flat were many rare eucalypts now fully grown, a secret abundance, mostly from the Northern Territory and flowering in a mass of gaudy asterisks. Even Ellen paused and gazed about.

It had been the graveyard of the less prepared suitors; Mr Cave though would have reeled off their names for her (in their evocative common parlance: Pumpkin Gum, Yellow Jacket, Barber's Gum, Kakadu Woollybutt, Manna Gum, Gympie Messmate, Bastard Tallowwood, and so on); except Ellen never wanted to hear the name of another eucalypt again.

Across her path was a long mulga snake, seeking warmth, which Ellen stepped around.

Why she had wandered so far from the house she couldn't say. It hadn't exactly been conscious. At last she stopped at a delicate mallee sprouting thin trunks, more like thin branches shoved into the ground.

If he now comes to me, where I am standing here, she decided, he must be following me. Aside from anything else it would show the *lengths* he would go to for her. And she wanted to see him.

Most of his stories, she began to realise, were about daughters and marriage; and these stories, she saw, she thought, were more and more directed at her.

It was enough for her not to think about the inevitable advance of Mr Cave.

The workman's shirt and slacks verging on the drab failed to neutralise her speckled beauty. If anything they made it still more startling. In fact, anyone coming upon her would conclude that if she was inconsolable it was to do with her beauty.

She immediately noticed his hair wet and he had evidently dried himself with his shirt.

"I am here," she called out.

For a good ten minutes they sat, almost touching at several points, without saying anything. Such ease of familiarity calmed her. It also turned her thoughts directly to him. Now when he began talking he was almost as indecisive as the Barber's Gum sprouting all over the place, behind them; he took his cue from it, his words slowly circling and searching, to enter her, and nobody else.

There was talk of a story ("Did you ever happen to hear . . . ?") from Mauritania, of all places, a vast desert country of medieval habits where, it is said, no building is more than two storeys high. In a stony part of this country, near some low mountains, a young long-haired woman was held captive by *an ogre*. He was a violent perspiring figure, easily angered. He lived in a stone hut with stone furniture; it also had stone windows. The young woman thought constantly of ways to escape. Obviously the best chance was at night, but the ogre had thought of that and slept with her hair in his teeth. She began to despair, though she never lost her beauty. One moonless night a thief got in, and carefully began removing her hair one by one from the monster's teeth. It took all night. Just as it became light he removed the last hair and they made their escape; and as they ran over the stony ground the young thief saw before him the pale beauty he had only heard rumours of, and she in her happiness at being free turned and saw her rescuer, the thief, for the first time.

Ellen had listened without moving.

Expecting him to go on or at least glance at her, Ellen found instead he was looking straight ahead, as if avoiding her.

Still on the subject he went on, choosing his words, like the thief removing the filaments of hair, carefully enough for Ellen to sit up and notice.

The relationship between a woman and her hairdresser, he began by pointing out, is intimate. It is said that women tell their hairdressers things they wouldn't dream of telling their husbands.

To exaggerate his bewilderment he gave a discreet cough.

Seated at the mirror a woman puts herself in the hands of the hairdresser, very often a male. It is an occasion, almost ceremonial; it is concentrated, partly sombre. The woman is robed. Hair is the only changeable part of the face. And it is hair that frames – and makes distinctive – the various concepts of feminine beauty. Shorn of hair a woman is reduced to essentials: hence, the all-too-appropriate symbolism of a woman having her head shorn before being paraded for sleeping with the enemy.

At the hairdresser a woman sees herself in the mirror at different stages of exposure. Behind her, at each stage, remains the hairdresser. First, the woman is washed and rinsed back to plainness; it is what she all along suspected. From there she follows with a critical-hopeful eye her transformation. The hairdresser becomes accustomed to tears. Even when the woman is satisfied with the result, she is also dissatisfied knowing her new appearance has been *acquired*, based as it is on illusion, an artful adjustment in the cutting, or an expansion in midair, as it were. Every woman has a firm opinion on the hair of others. Hair is power. In history as certain women gain in ascendancy, so too their hairdressers.

"Shoes and your hair. You can forget all that's in between," a greying woman behind sunglasses told Ellen on a bus in Sydney.

On that long street to the city, Oxford Street, Ellen had once tried a salon decorated in silver paint and candelabra while her father wandered up and down outside; and now she was hearing this man seated beside her, telling about a grazier's daughter visiting Sydney, a story of how power was transferred from the hairdresser to an innocent woman.

Her name was Catherine. She was from one of those old Riverina families, roots going way back. Fine homestead. The property was on the Murrumbidgee River, and the paddocks held so many sheep they looked, from certain angles, permed. Catherine's parents were separated, at least geographically; the mother who was still remembered as a flapper in Sydney society was naturally bored out of her mind in the Riverina and spent most of the year in Sydney, where she had an apartment in the Spanish style, at Elizabeth Bay. There she concentrated on charity work, light luncheons, improving her golf handicap, not always in that order. Every year in February, Sydney's month of lassitude and perspiration, she went to Europe. She had a grim, sun-battered beauty; large sums were regularly invested in clothes and cosmetics; she had some good jewellery in bank vaults.

At eighteen Catherine was taken by her father on regular trips to Sydney, and left there with her mother. It had been the mother's idea: the thought of her daughter vegetating in the country, surrounded by bleating sheep and the croaking of crows, and the blundering advances of the local yokels, was really too much to bear. Sydney would get her off horses and into cocktail dresses, even with those shoulders.

On the very first of these visits – for the yearling sales – Catherine's mother took one look at her, and phoned Maurice of Double Bay to have her daughter's hair fixed. And that became the routine whenever Catherine set foot in town.

It was difficult for a normal woman to gain entry to Maurice's, let alone at a day's notice. A woman had to be somebody, or look as if she were the ghost of somebody, or show a strong chance one day of being a somebody (via marriage, money or divorce).

Some women were too terrified to step inside Maurice's. Although he never smiled, he pulled an incredible number of faces, feminine in their intensities, mostly in the vicinity of grimaces, which were then multiplied by the glitzy mirrors. He also had a loud voice. His most common phrase was, "And what is *this*?" Sometimes he would give a woman's hair a withering flick with his fingertips. He had a row of five assistants which he supervised by clapping and rushing past and pointing, like a chess grandmaster in a demonstration match against a row of young hopefuls, and there was always one of them ready to pour him another Turkish coffee in the same tiny cup.

Such public tyranny would not of course have been tolerated if his eye was unreliable. Women though grew still when he stood behind and held their hair in the palm of his hands, as if weighing gold, then with a grimace made a rapid decision, cut here or curl or colour. "OK?" In his hands angry-looking women, angry to the point of ugly, were softened towards a regal "looking-down" appearance, depending a lot on age and amount of hair to play with. Others he made into what appeared to be splendid galleons, and to young blondes he supplied, via hair, the lightness and mobility of skiffs. For all his histrionic severity Maurice listened and offered sympathy whenever the subject turned to a problem more personal than hair. From all over the eastern suburbs – suburbs with names like Vaucluse, Bellevue Hill, Point Piper – women headed for his salon next to the Swiss shoe and handbag shop in Double Bay, and some were known to double-park in the middle of the street, anything not to be late for an appointment.

Catherine knew none of this.

She was a plain thing, who looked as if she was sitting outside under a tree.

Her mother clearly was a special client of Maurice's. With a grand gesture he entrusted the washing of Catherine's hair to his most promising apprentice, not much older than Catherine, who was single-mindedly pioneering the return to Sydney of long, shaved sideburns. His name was Tony Blacktin. He also swept the floors. As he spoke, Catherine looked at him in the mirror. He began by loudly imitating Maurice, which came out automatically as a sort of careless bluntness. Catherine sat quietly. He was perhaps unsuitable for a career in hairdressing. And Blacktin: where did that name come from?

Unexpectedly he asked Catherine, "I've been thinking of trying a moustache. What do you think?" Before she could answer he said, "The boss'd give me the sack."

He went on, "I was born in Sheffield. How about you?"

Encouraged by the softness of Catherine's attention he told things about his family. His mother was allergic to peaches, and was always late. The father used to grind his teeth, "You're going to be late for your own funeral!" He tried selling ice-cream from a van in Liverpool, but shot through from the wife and kids, and was last heard of playing a piano in a nightclub somewhere in Burma. Another Blacktin – a certain Cyril – was supposed to be brainy. He was a scientist who always sent his latest book around, wrapped in a brown paper bag.

He was still rattling away like this as Catherine leaned back and closed her eyes. Hot water flowed over her skull. Strong fingers encouraged the rinsing of her heavy wet hair.

Almost immediately, the fingers in her hair hesitated; and Catherine realised he had stopped talking.

She had just come in from the country, and hadn't even had time to change her dress.

The apprentice hairdresser was gazing into the rinsing basin, pressed against her neck. Dust rinsing to lazy brown river water swirled into the basin where it rose to the level of dam water, pale brown as if translucent in sunlight, and the water in the basin was warm and dam-shaped too. A residue of pale sand settled at the bottom.

Such country-brown water never made an appearance in the urban environment; certainly not in the salon at Double Bay. To the young apprentice who also swept the floor it spoke of space, summer paddocks, isolated trees. Moving his hands in the muddy water he expected to come up against a yabby or a gumleaf.

More and more images of swaying grass and dryness presented themselves through the country water which flowed from her through her hair. He thought she still had her eyes closed, as all women did. He kept his hand on her wet head; he could have stayed there all day. She had always been friendly to him.

As for Catherine she found him amusing. He was different. Some might find his face a bit bumpy and side-burned; but in the mirror Catherine saw an attractive faltering firmness. It became a habit whenever she visited Sydney to go straight to the salon, where Tony could hardly wait to wash and rinse her hair.

To make an appointment Catherine now posted the family's embossed cards and asked for Mr Blacktin.

He hardly knew whether he had fallen for her, or the river, or the idea of the brown country that flowed through her hair. After some hesitation she began going out with him for small meals and afterwards to a bar where he told more stories of his family and travels, as well as stories he'd heard from others; he even made some up: anything to amuse her, to keep her attention. And because of the intervals between visits, Catherine found she was looking forward to seeing him and hearing his voice almost as much as the city itself. Besides, she hardly knew anyone else in Sydney.

After about a year, the story goes, Catherine sat in the chair once more and said to him, "I want it all short, cut it as short as you can."

Either she expected him to follow her in every way, or she wanted to cut the amount of country dust in her hair; a side benefit might have been to give her mother a cautionary jolt.

Now Blacktin was forbidden by Maurice to be a cutter – that honour was reserved for poets wielding tiny scissors after years of arduous training – and as Maurice strode by on one of his supervisory sweeps he saw his apprentice, elbows splayed and tongue protruding like a man painting a white line between bricks, and took in at a glance Catherine's completely altered appearance and the heaps of pale brown hair at the foot of her chair. Tony was so busy he didn't notice Maurice standing behind him or in the mirror. Catherine did; and the way she met his eyes calmly made him move on, without saying a word.

Maurice was a subtle man. From a distance he remained looking at the pair for several minutes, Catherine and his apprentice sporting the absurd sideburns.

They were happy together. Anticipation coloured their intimacy. It was at a far deeper level than the usual intimacy enjoyed by hairdressers, he saw. They were young, and he envied their innocence. Nevertheless, he went into his tiny office and, after briefly looking at his hands, telephoned Catherine's mother, strengthening the already useful loyalty between them.

25

Forrestiana

A SHORT TREE, ornamental.
In Western Australia people grow them in gardens for the splash of Maranello-red flowers.

Short enough for it to be damned in some circles as a *shrub*.

Some years ago . . . in a town not far from Melbourne, its name similar to the one that stonkered Sherlock Holmes, a thin woman with a pointy nose lived with her father, the town's solicitor.

Her name was Georgina Bell.

In her early thirties, Georgina travelled for the first and only time to Europe. These were the days when Australians fled from their empty country in bulging P&O liners – similar in sensation to the driving horizontality of trains, except on sloppy deep liquid.

A strange thing happened on the ship.

At Port Said, where the heat suddenly became stationary, she stepped on to land. There she became channelled, compressed, sleeve-tugged and urgently shouted at by hundreds of beggars, hawkers, hangers-on and children in torn shirts; it was absolute bedlam. In amongst it all one brown face stood out and stared at her.

He followed her into the bazaar. But there the noise and the smells, these people who wouldn't leave her alone – it was all too much. Returning to the ship she went to her cabin and tried to rest in the heat. Almost immediately she sat up to find the same man seated by her bunk. His eyes were fixed on her. He had slightly moist, fleshy lips, a faint aroma of cloves.

Outside came the murmuring hum of the foreign place. He probably didn't know a word of English, she thought afterwards. From his blouse he pulled out a live chicken, like a magician. Unsmiling he stroked it. Slowly he reached out and laid it on her thigh where it remained, as if hypnotised.

There and then he could have done anything to her. But the ship's crew burst in; she could never understand how or why they did.

After a month in England, Georgina Bell returned home. As she replied to anyone who asked, "London of course was fascinating, but I missed my father and the garden".

The family house was an old bluestone, with rosebuds, urns and arbours.

Before her trip Georgina had paid only polite attention to her father's senior partner, a married man with a neat moustache and four children. Now she noticed that the things he said were unusual and very often amusing to her. Several times when she accompanied him to other towns for conveyancing work they dined together. To Georgina's surprise, and after faint resistance, she became his lover.

Georgina could hardly believe what happened. She felt a sudden overflowing fullness and a rapidly reaching depth of gentleness and concern for all things to do with him. She tried to put it into words, but only laughed. With him she could ask or say anything; never had she been so close to anyone. She had a very clear idea of his appearance; at the same time it was vague! She wanted to see him all the time, but could not. They could only snatch moments together. She wanted to knit him things, buy him a necktie and underwear; she would have seen to it that his shoes were properly shining. Georgina wondered if his wife of twenty years understood him as well as she did. It was painful to see him seated with her in church, just across the aisle, with their children. There, and in her father's office, they could display only an extreme politeness towards each other.

For almost two years they remained lovers. Without warning, on an ordinary Saturday afternoon, he fell and died in the street. He wasn't even overweight. Georgina could not tell them – her father, anyone in the town – they were lovers. In public she could not even show her grief. "And the earth levelled over him." He was buried in the garden, there in the shadow of hawthorn.

Day after day Georgina wanted to shriek.

Over his grave she planted flowers, their fine roots reaching down into his body. Every day Georgina wore them on her bosom, red fuchsias, and placed some in a vase by her bed.

These strong colours she could proudly show in public; and in time she seemed to grow better.

26

Platyphylla

SLOWLY THEY BEGAN leaving the Fuchsia Gum.

The careful way he told the solicitor's story suggested it had actually happened, and Ellen saw Georgina Bell as a woman pale in disabled browns, and her elongated nose, a chalk dipped in red ink, and wondered how after that a woman could possibly rearrange herself. There was also the father in his considerable vertical dignity. She had a rush of questions to ask.

Alongside, this man now and then brushed against her hip and shoulder – he probably wasn't even aware of it.

She saw into the distance he had a gentle side; yet there was nothing gentle in the way he was finishing the stories abruptly, at the very moment she wanted to know more. It matched her present situation, which could only be described as suspended, unsatisfied. This apparent gentleness of his might have been little more than a necessary politeness, a stepping back a few paces. After all, here he was most days in among the trees with her, a woman; the two of them, nobody else around.

She wanted to talk to him.

"We have more smiles today. What is it?"

Holding the smile, though it felt more like a frown, she met his eye.

The Fuchsia Gum had been planted outside Ellen's window as an "ornamental". For the first time he was strolling with her on the gravel past the front door. At any moment her father could appear around the corner – with Mr Cave. It was enough for Ellen to become riddled with a sort of reckless gaiety. "That's where I sleep," she said.

She wasn't sure whether he'd heard. All his attention seemed to be taken suddenly by a rather plain Red Mallee (*E. socialis*).

It was almost maddening he was now spending so much time with her, in and out of trees, without her knowing exactly why. To Ellen he felt like a perpetual warm wind which exerted a steady pleasant sort of pressure over different parts of her body, pressing her dress against the hollows; and the way too he easily changed the subject was like the wind, the way it simply shifted direction, at the same time constantly surrounding her.

Still in the vicinity of low-height eucalypts he went on to mention, in a thoughtful voice, how in an outer suburb of Hobart an actuary with a well-known insurance company needed a stepladder to woo a widow who passed by his house every day, to and from work. To attract her attention, the story went, he set about pruning his enormous front hedge and umbrella pine into truly amazing animal shapes, the way certain tropical birds go to exhausting lengths to build and decorate elaborate nests or perform strenuous somersaults against the sky. The lengths to which a male will go to catch the eye of the difficult-to-please female, he was saying.

The trouble was that a display of an obsession in the form of romantic hedge-cutting attracted the wrong sort of people, said he. From all parts of Hobart, and the mainland of Australia, and the work-ethic states of Asia they came by the busload: people with cameras. But the widow, how did she respond?

Ellen couldn't help smiling at his incredulous tone, but she was preoccupied by too many questions; and there and then she decided that instead of strolling on through the trees until he decided to leave, *branching off* in that way of his – in the same abrupt way he finished his stories – she would turn on her heel, and return to the house. "I'll have to be getting back."

Not intending to hurry she crossed the gravel drive. In the distance she saw her father and the unmistakable larger figure of Mr Cave near the windbreak, Mr Cave appearing suddenly to pause and turn back and point up; reaching the front door Ellen was struck by a fit of helpless hiccupping, which would have appeared from behind only as weeping.

The single White Gum stood back from the hidden bend, near the swimming place Ellen imagined was her secret. There behind the thumping great River Reds it offered a flash of porcelain whiteness, like a curtain parting, revealing a woman's generous bare legs.

Ellen had stayed in her room all morning. She heard the murmurings of her father and Mr Cave. By week's end he would be finished naming the last few trees. Ellen noticed her father avoided her face. It had been an arduous trial for him too. And now before him was the prospect of an empty house.

Ellen heard the door slam as her father and the almost-there suitor set out.

She changed from a dress into shirt and trousers, and back again into another dress. In between she gazed into the mirror. She saw herself in different shoes. There was never enough light in her bedroom! Still, this body glowing with a pale completeness she accepted.

It always surprised her that whenever she went out among the trees he managed to find her. It was as if he had many hands. Would he come from the left or right, or from behind? She never knew. At any moment he could drop down in front of her from one of the trees, like Errol Flynn or Tarzan.

It was now long past the hour she normally left the house. Shadows had begun their fold-out from the other side of trees. The cotton of her dress felt warm all over, as if freshly ironed.

Ellen strode towards the river, into the concentration of her father's trees. Near the swimming place she slowed. This man who was interested enough to find her day after day: to think that yesterday she'd simply turned her back and walked away. What would he make of that? What if now he never bothered appearing again – what then?

The water was clear, the furry sticks and stones along the bottom appeared magnified. Patterned by the over-arching branches the hot light tattooed her arms, and as Ellen entered the water she imagined her face dappled tortoiseshell too. She felt a spreading liquid affinity with the flow of nature. It was a truth found easily in a river. The river-flow gently pushed against her, a patient pressure that would always prevail, a true insistence, and Ellen splashed and drifted and splashed again, idly thinking of him, happy at the thought that what she was allowing could hardly be wrong.

Ellen's body made a startling appearance among the trees. It was pale and all-over soft, whereas the trunks surrounding her were nothing but hard. The warm handful of hair between her legs and the rest of her softness was how animals, such as rabbits, can be seen against rocks.

Facing the sun Ellen felt herself peeled open, at least to the eye. Idly she touched her hair to see if it had dried. Later she twisted to inspect her heel. Ellen had nothing else to do, so she stayed.

Surrounded on all sides by immovable grey trunks she couldn't remember where exactly she'd left her clothes.

It was then she heard footsteps. He seemed to be treading on all the discarded strips of bark he could find. Ellen turned and faced him. Aware of her nakedness she was not fully conscious of her speckled beauty.

At arm's length he stopped.

She wanted him immediately to begin another story, perhaps thinking it would cover her nakedness, even though he was looking slightly away. Over one arm she noticed her yellow dress and other things.

"I remember once . . . " Changing his mind he turned.

His hand simply came forward and for the first time touched her cheek, and moved up to her clammy hair.

"Why did you run away yesterday?"

Ellen shook her head, and apparently raised her arm too; for without warning his head went down, and gave a gentle animal *bite* on her arm, enough to leave a mark.

"I could have been talking too much," he frowned. "I may have got carried away."

As he began dressing her from the top down, one item at a time, leaving her half-dressed while holding up her remaining underclothes, Ellen felt a tremble of concentration, and didn't care if he noticed. She looked down at his ears and neck.

She raised her arms for him to lower the dress.

Concentrating on the large buttons he squatted in front of her. And Ellen began feeling soft and warm, ready too. Briefly she considered the woman he called Georgina, the one in the constricted cabin, the warm chicken pressed against her thigh.

Behind them rustled the river, endless silk over pebbles.

There are always children lost in a forest. A single foot is struck by an arrow, bitten by a snake, or the heel is bruised, the slipper falls off. Certain boots are endowed with magical striding properties. Every beautiful princess has an evil stepmother. Well illustrated is the woman with three breasts, one for each man in her life.

"In a white flat-roofed house in Drummoyne," he was saying, giving up on the buttons and looking around for her shoes, "lived an international authority on aerodynamics, with three tall daughters. His name was along the lines of Shaw-Gibson, DFC. A man with a moustache: he should have been knighted. Young men used to troop around to his house, not so much to see his daughters but to try lifting the small meteorite he had displayed on his sideboard.

"Would you prefer him or Mr Clem Sackler who had the dandruff? Clem Sackler was a small man with ginger eyebrows who lived alone in a terrace house in Darlinghurst. Well, not exactly alone."

Ellen had decided not to help him in any way at all. Her nakedness had made her supreme.

"In Australia after the war, when men and women wore hats, it was also the custom to have a large aviary in the backyard filled with small birds, and if not an aviary then a cage on the back porch containing a deafening parrot. In time this custom – which raises all sorts of questions – was replaced by an obsession with tropical fish in tanks, and for a brief moment it was all the rage to have an angora rabbit in the backyard.

"Clem Sackler had canaries. At any given time dozens of the little things fluttered and trilled in cages in different rooms of his house. Some days they could be heard from the footpath. As soon as he arrived home from his job at the railways he set about replenishing their food and water, and at intervals let selected ones out for exercise. That was Clem Sackler's life."

After abruptly examining one of Ellen's toes he continued.

"As a breeder, Sackler had a small reputation among connoisseurs. For years he had been trying to breed a white canary. All his hopes rested on a pampered hyperactive male, grey with streaks of buff. In the layers of his feathers Sackler saw a flash of white. The other canaries were green or yellow, and shared cages in the front sleep-out, where louvres opened onto the frangipani, and in the kitchen more cages were stacked on top of each other, like small skyscrapers. He must have had fifty or sixty birds.

"The grey male occupied a large cage with its own mirror in Sackler's upstairs bedroom."

As he traced his finger along her foot, Ellen began smiling almost happily. The thought of the many little birds.

"One evening in summer, Sackler came home dog-tired. As always he went upstairs and opened the cage for the grey bird to have its vital exercise. Then he lay down on his bed and gazed up at the ceiling. It needed a coat of paint. The whole place was falling down. He ran his tongue over the front of his teeth. Briefly he whistled a few notes out of tune, a habit from living with so many canaries. As he lay there in the heat he saw how his life, at least the last ten years, had been subdivided into too many small units – the many different little birds – which were impersonal, concerned only with food and chirping among themselves. His life appeared to have a pattern. In fact, it had no single focus.

"It was a revelation to the 'canariologist'.

"He got up and raised the window. He must have been half-asleep. No sooner had he felt the breeze than he gave a hoarse cry and slammed the window shut – but too late. Flying around the room his grey canary had darted at the opportunity and, grazed by the slamming window, escaped.

"From the balcony there was no sign of the bird. Sackler ran downstairs and hurried up and down the street, squinting up at the gutters and under cars, and into the small front yards – concreted and taken up with old motorbikes, in that part of Sydney.

"Over the next few days he walked the streets, knocking on doors, searching the most likely places. He left a note in the window of the flyblown delicatessen where he bought his cigarettes. After a week of this he began to wonder if he knew anything at all about the habits of the canary. He began to accept its loss. It had probably been taken by a cat."

He yawned. Ellen saw the broad expanse of jaw. He could have slept at her feet there and then. She almost reached out and touched his hair. But he continued the very sad story of the breeder of canaries.

"One Friday evening Mr Clem Sackler was walking home from Kings Cross. It was dark. Not far from his street a few terrace houses had their lights on; people were sitting at tables, moving about. One window was partly obscured by a tree. At first he thought the rapid movement was a fruit-bat – they're all around East Sydney, Darlinghurst – but this movement had been inside the white room. A woman was seated at a piano and, as she began playing, the same fluttering blur appeared again, careering around to the music, before gently landing on the woman's shoulder. Sackler went to the window. He couldn't believe his eyes.

"The woman stood up from the piano, and turned her back. She had a small waist and hair pulled into a bun. With his lost bird perched on her shoulder, she left the room.

"Sackler went straight to the front door and was about to ring.

"The bell was polished brass. There was a doormat the same sandy colour as his eyebrows. Camellias were flowering in two large tubs. And the windows had neat curtains.

"Below the bell was printed HEIDE KIRSCHNER, PIANO.

"The next morning he returned. From several houses away he could hear the piano. It seemed she never stopped playing. Through the window he saw the woman seated alongside a pupil, pointing to the sheet music and demonstrating. As he watched he saw the grey canary land on her shoulder.

"Sackler went away. He had to think about this. He was forty-eight. Whenever he returned to the house his bird was on her shoulder. Finally, he rang the bell. His suit had been dry-cleaned, he wore a tie; that same day he was seated alongside Miss Kirschner, learning to play the piano.

"Did the grey canary recognise him? It clung to Miss Kirschner, and seemed to glare at him! Canaries love the various rhythms of music, she told him, who was supposed to be an expert on canaries. Even Bach, she smiled. She played the beginning of a fugue, and Sackler followed his bird as it tore around the room, and returned to the shoulder of Miss Kirschner.

"Sackler soon liked the sound of her strong accent, and her earnestness with all things musical, so he couldn't help staring when she broke into a childlike gaiety.

"It took two months of piano lessons before the bird landed on his shoulder. By then he had mastered the scales and with terrible clumsiness was attempting simple melodies. His teacher had deep, deep reserves of patience."

Still in her state of half-undress, Ellen felt a dreamy

contentment. It was always like this under a tree listening to stories. She realised she was smiling.

"In that time," he continued, "the canary-breeder had an almost daily view of the perfect paleness of Miss Kirschner's arms." He lifted Ellen's elbow. "In all his days he had never seen such skin, so fine and smooth her entire arms blended into the ivory keys. He couldn't take his eyes off her bare arms. One small bite," he cleared his throat, "would have left a permanent mark."

"I'm listening," said Ellen.

"By now the canary sometimes chose his shoulder, other times hers. Miss Kirschner tried to encourage the bird to nibble her pupil's ear. It was time he made a decision. After the lessons now she served small cakes soaked in honey on blue plates, and enquired after his health. On days she wore a high embroidered blouse or a special brooch she demanded his opinion. More and more Sackler felt the attraction of habit, of merely dropping in, to be there, never mind the lessons.

"Still, he only had to glance down at Miss Kirschner's alabaster skin, and back to the frisky male bird, for his resolve – his reason for being there – to return.

"And so on a Sunday evening, when she left the room, talking as she went, he lifted the canary from his shoulder. He put it struggling in his coat pocket, and let himself out.

"As he passed the window the brightly lit room with the piano was still empty. He kept his hand in his pocket wrapped around the bird. That way he hurried home.

"Upstairs he returned the canary to its cage. For some time then he lay on his bed. He went back over the night he had first looked into the pianist's room, saw the bird flying about like a moth, noticed her narrow waist. She too lived alone. He wondered what she was doing just then. If it was bewildering for her, it had been bewildering for him as well. With the bird safely back in its cage he could consider which of the females downstairs were most suitable to mate with the male. Clearly he had been doing something wrong; it hadn't worked. Downstairs the chirping of the different canaries sounded curiously muted after Miss Kirschner's piano playing.

"Next morning, waking early, Clem Sackler removed the dressing gown he'd always draped at night over the cage. On the metal floor lay the grey male on its side, dead."

Ellen walked up and down.

"Where did you hear that? What an awful story. I feel sorry for someone like that. I think you've made it up." Ellen stopped in front of him. "Is it true?"

Here he could look at her closely. He began wandering among the many different birthmarks and beauty spots. As for Ellen, her questions seemed to direct him towards her state of dress. For a moment, without looking down, Ellen wasn't sure whether she was being buttoned or unbuttoned.

Came his voice, "When the breeder of canaries knocked on Miss Kirschner's door he had dandruff on his shoulders. She had a squint in one eye – something like that. And she had the excruciating taste in furnishings usually found with musicians. It's a mystery how an attraction can spring up in one person for another. Who can say why? It would be amazing, except it happens all the time. A person's voice, say a man's voice, heard in the dark or behind a door is sometimes enough. But it must be a combination of things. What do you think?"

"Just voice isn't enough, I don't believe."

"There must be cases where the attraction is not deliberate. It just sort of happens," he proposed. "It can't be explained – a real mystery. There's no logic to it," he added. It was enough for him to shake his head.

"Logic?" She almost wanted to laugh.

"I mean the person is not given a choice in the matter."

In and out went the conversation, and the light and shade slanted between the trees. Normally he would have gone long ago. Clearly he wanted to stay. Frowning again, he was looking away from her.

"And you don't know whether your stories are true or not?" She waited, not thinking of anything else.

So it was left in that intimate, unresolved state, which too can be seen as something of a mystery.

27

Diversicolor

IN A SMALL town out west of Sydney a Greek owned a café in the main street. It was divided down the middle into booths with fixed tables, a glass dish on the tables holding the slices of white bread. The walls had been painted the colour of the sea, and near the cappuccino machine a photograph torn from a magazine showed a white monastery perched on a barren cliff.

The Greek's wife did the cooking out the back, his daughter waited on the tables, and he sat all day behind the cash register, keeping his eye on things.

This daughter wore her black hair long, and blouses with a low neckline – sometimes it was a T-shirt. She never wore a dress or a skirt. She seemed discontented. She scarcely said a word.

The Greek had moved his family inland, as far from the sea as possible. This was to prevent his daughter being seen in a bathing costume. It was rumoured that a part of her body was disfigured by a wine-dark stain, though no one – certainly none of the hoons who sat around every night in the café – had seen such a mark with their own eyes.

There was never much going on in town. The few young men who remained spent the most vital years of their lives talking about cars and hazarding guesses about the waitress, only to clam up and grin when she came to their table. If one of them was lucky enough to take her to the pictures or for a drive to the next town her father wanted her home by 11 p.m., and she herself never allowed anyone to see what lay underneath her blouse and jeans. She'd grown up with these young men. She knew only too well the way they thought and talked, and how their hair would always be combed and look the same.

One morning a man no one had seen before sat in one of the booths and ordered a breakfast.

He had big ears and a small head. He wore a tie. To occupy himself he spent a good ten minutes trying to balance the menu on the lid of the bread dish.

This man took one look at the long-haired waitress and began taking breakfast there every morning, and gave the same elaborate instructions on how to turn the eggs, thinking it might amuse her, which she ignored.

He was staying at the hotel. He had always been a talker. He could talk about any subject you cared to name. He especially liked introducing himself to a woman, and going from there. He found that his incredible ugliness wasn't a handicap. In fact, it may have helped. He was a good listener. Even when he was young he was "as cunning as fifty crows". He had started out selling cough-cures door to door, then it was vacuum cleaners, and Singer sewing machines. On the side he was on commission for a manufacturer of flagpoles, who'd recently diversified into stepladders –

difficult things to move in large numbers. He always looked hungry. The usual laws of disappointment apply more to a travelling salesman than to most other men.

He'd been attracted to the sullenness of the waitress, and when he asked around and heard she had something on her body so zealously guarded no man had managed to report its details he decided he would not leave town until he had seen it for himself.

With this in mind he took all his meals at the Greek's. At night he made sure he was the last to leave, even if it meant ordering another coffee. But he soon found the technique which had given him such success across dozens of country towns – namely, outrageous flattery and obviously absurd exaggeration, and the same old jokes, while fixing his eyes on the woman in question – was getting him nowhere. The waitress showed no interest. If anything, she became downright suspicious, hostile even.

After a week of rejection he decided to give himself one more night; he couldn't stay in this dump forever. The decision came as easily as ordering another toast. He left his suitcase on the bed and set out for the café. In the dark a woman in a black shawl appeared in front of him. She was an old woman he hadn't seen before. "It's not the end of the world," she seemed to be saying, grabbing at his sleeve. She had forgotten to put in her teeth. Taking his hand she rubbed it with her fingers, and pointed. "Become an upright citizen, all ears."

At least that's how it sounded – either a riddle or a scornful screech. As he turned away with a good-natured laugh he tripped over and grazed his knee.

It was the waitress with her customary tired look who noticed. She actually spoke, "What have you been doing?"

And looking down he found splinters all over his hands.

After that he noticed the Greek and his daughter glancing at him. Unexpectedly the father nodded and smiled. But it was too late. The man had already decided what to do. Without trying to win her over on that last night he finished eating and didn't even order a coffee. He waited outside for the place to close. There wasn't anybody around. When her bedroom light came on he went behind the café.

Carefully he climbed the picket fence. He felt like whistling a little tune. Why hadn't anyone else done this before? There was a loquat tree, a fowl yard, bits of wood. At the louvred window he stood on tiptoe.

In her room the young waitress was stepping out of the last brief piece of clothing. Casually she turned. He almost gasped at the bulging strength of her nakedness; the rich tangle of black below the hips.

To see more he stretched: and there he saw it on her legs, a dark stain, as if she was up to her knees in ink.

At that moment she faced the window. Although she didn't cry out, he stepped back; or so he thought. Something solid met him from behind. He couldn't move. There was no point in struggling. He could still see into the room and the waitress's pale body. His arms disappeared into his sides. And he felt himself merge into something altogether hard and straight; unusually tall. Foolishly, he realised he should be getting back to his home in Sydney. His head became cold. He then began to hear voices.

From the waitress's muscular legs the stain was transferred across the short distance of chicken wire, bottles and tins, lengths of useful timber, etc., over the grey splintered fence to the base of the new telegraph pole, Karri, which would stand in all weathers with a clear view of the Greek waitress in her room, regularly naked.

She of course lived happily ever after, sometimes enjoying the company of men.

28

Decipiens

TO THIS DAY examples continue of a man coming across a woman undressed who is simply unable to avert, let alone shut, his eyes. Very common within the species. At any given moment it happens somewhere in the world. Accidental? More than likely an essential deep-seated mechanism is at work here; and as the eyes possess the unprotected body, a secondary mechanism is activated which can produce unexpected consequences, on occasions, retribution.

29

Neglecta

Two DAYS HAD passed: and no sign of him. To Ellen the encyclopaedic landscape took on a completely blank and sullen appearance.

Nothing much moved, at least nothing out of the ordinary; no figure seen coming towards her.

On the third, winds and slanting rain came from the east and whiplashed the eucalypts into helpless shrubs, a panorama of dented reputations, great trees shivering and flinching in feminine distress, some split or uprooted, while a small paddock of pale brown grass was combed into a vast mat, the sort of orange-haired mat found outside certain hairdressing salons in Sydney.

Made jagged by the wind Ellen began having restless, irrational thoughts. Now he was gone. What had got into her? As she kept thinking she frowned. Turning towards him naked that day at the river she had felt an extreme, open simplicity. It was also trust in him. In a sense she had already given herself; hardly could be seen as a stranger now.

Waiting at the places where they usually met she immediately knew he wouldn't be there. She went further afield, wandering, tree to tree.

Eucalypts, selfish trees, give precious little shelter. On one of those days Ellen was a long way from the house, and perhaps wishing the dripping gums had the umbrella qualities of oaks, or ordinary plane trees, or even gloomy Teutonic pines, became wet through, forgetting to button up her stockman's coat. It was true that with her hair plastered across her forehead and ears, and having just hurried a zigzag course, water still running down her face, she felt at the centre of a possibly sad drama; she wore a determined, set expression. Why else remove her wet dress and place it on the mysterious nail in the trunk of her tree? Without thinking, she'd come across the *E. maidenii* – and there was the nail. Hanging to dry, the dress repeated a collapsed version of herself.

At least the weather brought a halt to Mr Cave's implacable march. Out of habit, though, he still arrived in the morning, stamping his muddy boots on the verandah, he and Holland. Each gripping a mug of tea they contemplated the dirty weather.

Only the far triangular paddock remained, of mostly stringybarks, containing at its point closest to town the one and only Ghost Gum. The ornamentals lining the drive up to the house he was leaving to last. Apparently the idea was to name the last forty eucalypts in a sort of triumphant sweep up to the front door. Mr Cave told Holland he needed another day, two at the most.

Ellen heard this over and above the rain on the iron roof as she brushed past on the verandah, without a dress under her waterproof, and almost stumbled.

Everybody but Ellen could see Mr Cave was about to win

her hand. Incredibly, she had again concentrated all her thoughts and energies elsewhere, in another person out there somewhere, quite a compelling invisible man, perhaps hoping that by turning her head in the opposite direction the industrial advance of Mr Cave would somehow veer off and go away. There was little her father, or anybody else, could do to save her now.

When the weather cleared she went up into the tower and searched in all directions for any movement, any sign of him. Familiar things had shifted positions, others had left bits of themselves strewn on the ground, breaking the line of a fence, or else stood up at strange angles. Here and there hollows normally filled with shadow glittered with water; a landscape after a battle.

So trees produced oxygen in the form of words. Ellen could hear his voice. Stories with foreign settings came closer to home. They came back to her. It was due to sheets of water lying around, and the bedraggled eucalypts begging for attention.

Between stories Ellen had allowed him to reach out and help her quite unnecessarily over a fallen tree or rocks.

The River Peppermint (*E. elata*), it has more botanical names applied to it than any other eucalypt. "In one of the harbourside haciendas in Vaucluse lived a small bright-eyed woman in gold sandals who had been married and divorced so many times she had trouble remembering her current name. Other women liked her, and yet she was never happy. One day for no apparent reason a muscular man with a star tattooed on one shoulder and wearing nothing but boots, shorts and navy singlet dumped a load of wet yellow sand in her drive and – would you believe? – ambled up to the front door for a receipt. She was still in her dressing-gown, her hair a mess. It took a minute or two to sort out the confusion, only for it to be replaced as they remained looking at one another by an altogether different, deeper confusion which she recognised . . . "

As for the slender Steedman's Mallee (*E. steedmanii*) from the west, naturally Ellen anticipated something about larrikin jockeys or drovers; instead he brought up the sad case of the postman in Botany (a suburb of Sydney) who found the job of delivering mail *beneath him*, Ellen smiled, and performed his duties with such reluctance he was transferred to smaller and smaller country towns until he ended up in this very town just over the khaki river, where his sister served at the counter and he could occasionally be heard moving about or clearing his throat inside the office.

Trees with the most shameless histrionic common names, such as the Lemon Scented, Silver Princess, the various Yellow Jackets and the Wallangarra White dropping leaves in the dam, to mention four, wandered in and out of view which became memory. And Ellen felt his words circling closer; quite insistent, really.

There's a place called Corunna in north-west Spain, he had said. A place of rocks – geological delirium. Corunna is known for just two things: foul weather, it never stops raining, and its lighthouse built of granite in the Dark Ages. Local families call it "the Tower of Caramel". In this tower, the story goes, was housed a miraculous mirror that could reflect anything that happened anywhere in the world. The women of Corunna went to the mirror to see where their men were at any given moment, their hardships and dangers at sea, as well as births, deaths and marriages.

One Sunday a local man in a black suit went up to check on the woman he was meant to marry. Instead he found a young foreign woman with a strong jaw and broad hips consulting the mirror – at the suggestion of the local tourist office – to discover the whereabouts of her always exuberant girlfriend who had neglected to leave a forwarding address. The Spaniard was about to go when he saw clearly in the mirror his fiancée in the arms of the mayor's son! Beside the bed was a carafe of wine. As he stared his fiancée moved to be on top of the other one. The Spaniard turned to the startled Australian. "I'll kill them! Now!" He really meant it.

The no-nonsense Australian woman saw nothing in the mirror, not even a sign of her cheerful friend, and placed a soothing hand on his arm.

She was from Geelong. She was always leaving or coming back, as if she was attached to a very long length of elastic. First it was Bali. After that, India. She went to London and came back. South America was on her list. She went back to Europe, doing it on trains, using London as a base, before feeling the tug of home. On her return she would at once begin planning her next move.

To cut a long story short, he said, the young woman from Geelong and the Spaniard left the tower together, and were seen enjoying themselves in one of the cafés. She stayed on in Corunna. He came to her room. The dark sea that kept trying to squeeze in through the window and into her room, and the sounds of the seabirds and the foreign words outside, while inside this man with the blueish face gave her such solemn attention, his eyes and hands never stopping, combined with the energy of her youth to produce a sympathetic intensity – he had said – an intense spreading softness she had never experienced before.

In the room with him she measured her smooth good health and saw her life laid out ahead, sunlit, obeying the laws of perspective. Nevertheless, after a week she became restless again. In a mass of good-natured smiles she announced it was time for her to be leaving; the man showed his surprise by shouting at her. But she had decided, though when she looked back from the bus at his receding figure she felt confused and blew her nose.

In London at the most unexpected moments she saw the room in Corunna, which seemed from a distance to be jammed in at an angle among the black rocks. She kept seeing him across the room and close up. It was their room. He had a long face and hairs on his shoulders: she liked his solemn expression. She could feel his mouth and hear his voice.

A person meets thousands of different people across a lifetime, a woman thousands of different men, of all shades, and many more if she constantly passes through different parts of the world. Even so, of the many different people a person on average meets it is rare for one to fit almost immediately in harmony and general interest. For all the choices available the odds are enormous. The miracle is there to be grasped. Perhaps in unconscious recognition of this she had tugged both his ears early one morning in a rush of gaiety which he extended by making a great show of rolling on the floor in agony.

E. neglecta

In London she realised she should never have left. At strange important moments a person is given one and only one chance; and that had been one.

It was raining in Corunna. She hurried along the streets and tried the cafés. All the men could do was shrug. She gave descriptions of him. All morning she sat with a hot chocolate at their usual table. On the third day she went up to the mirror in the tower to find his whereabouts. There was nothing. The mirror was black.

As she turned to go she had a glimpse of herself – a figure almost like her, from behind. Remaining still she saw herself in the mirror fifteen, twenty years down the track. Alone, quite muscular in the legs, she was holding a heavy shopping bag with a bunch of celery sticking out: near her was a thin tree, not very tall, with dark green, somewhat patchy leaves.

Ellen made her way down from the tower.

There had been no sign of him. She realised she wasn't even sure of his name. What then about the near future? Too terrible to even think about: it was rushing towards her. On the other hand she didn't want her life to be a vast empty paddock.

In her room she felt as restless as the woman from Geelong, in his story.

She scribbled a note. "We must talk. I am your unhappy daughter." She shoved it under her father's door.

30

Papuana

CONSIDER THE BURDEN of being the first white woman born in New Guinea. Its debilitating effects can hardly be imagined by those luckily born looking like everybody else. Beginning as an incandescent child on the plantation, growing up there, to the boarding school in Brisbane, the various careers and romances after that, until marriage to the smartly dressed Italian, the faintly mental load she carried about can be likened to those of any number of island women condemned to spending their lives with a wide load of firewood or green bananas balanced on their heads.

If she was in Brisbane, she would be known by many people.

Large (seriously enormous), she took refuge in caftans and sunny florals, and wide-diameter earrings which swung and jangled whenever she moved. Her hair had gone from bottle-blonde to muddy-grey. For some reason, white skin does not belong in the tropics. Heat and humidity had battered her face and arms, though she had a lovely small smile. In Brisbane she ran a jewellery shop in one of the city malls. With no warning, and just when she had turned fifty, the husband left her for another woman. At around the same time the first of the melanomas were diagnosed on her cheek and neck. To their son, who had his own problems, what with a small family as well as his own retail business in a nearby mall, she gave instructions and made him promise – she had him swear on a Bible – that after her death he was to spread her ashes over the garden of her ex-husband, whom she hated.

A ghost story for another time.

31

Patellaris

HER FATHER HAD warned her about men. Did that include *fathers*?

Otherwise, men were known to be weak and evasive. A man could not be relied upon, not really; they were always somewhere else. And men were constantly trying to convince. It was as if that was their purpose for being on earth. Ellen had her face to the swirling wallpaper. They told stories, spoke with tongues as smooth as you like, and with the one thing in mind – still, it invariably alerted something pleasant in her. Always wanting to convince.

As for fathers, what about her own – the man now moving about in the other room?

Women he once described as "little engines". Speaking generally, that is; with just a touch of the usual exaspera-tion. Visualising heat, pipes and vibrations was easier than trying to understand them. Ellen had noticed that with women in town her father assumed an indifferent, often blunt manner, which they even found attractive.

In his room Holland was squatting over the plaques he'd had engraved for outdoor display, the names of all the eucalypts under the sun, sorting through them on the floor. Ellen came in, and when he didn't say anything she sat down.

It took a few minutes to become accustomed to the air in her father's room. And as always Ellen looked around with curiosity: at the absence of true softness, of colour – no mirror in the room. Instead, she followed the haphazard brownness of bits of equipment, instruments, machinery parts, the rain gauge spilling pencils; heavy coats, spare boots, the pioneer's camp stretcher; ledgers, papers, cigarette-rolling machine; suitcase, and the shotgun in the corner he said was ready loaded to keep the young bucks away; calendar showing the colossal Red Gum taking up an entire footpath in Adelaide – a gift at the beginning of the year, from Mr Cave.

The room presented a silent untidy harmony similar to a hillside of fallen trees. And yet it was *cavelike*. Ellen respected its differences, signs of her father's scattered self; a sort of random, long-established individuality.

"Talk about havoc," he was now saying, "complete mayhem. Any number of trees have been skittled. It'll never be the same."

"Dams are full, and I couldn't get near the river."

Her father nodded.

To one side he pushed the names of the weaker species, those split down the middle, uprooted, those with shallow roots.

"Our friend Mr Cave's out there having a quick dekko. Decent of him."

Ellen squatted beside him. "You can get replacements for all these. That won't be so difficult, will it?"

"It's difficult to make much headway in this business. It's taken all this time . . . And nature's always ready to step in. Nature's always leaning forward, very patient. Only the other day was an item in the paper about the eucalypt first seen by somebody, forget who, a hundred years ago. A description was recorded, it was given the name *rameliana*, but it was never seen again. I'm sure I've told you about this. Over the years it's become one of the mystery trees. Mr Cave was even asking the other day whether it had ever existed. But now I read in the paper an expedition has come across a surviving specimen – in the desert, west of the Olgas." He nodded at the thought. "That would have been one to get our hands on."

Gazing at the back of her father's neck Ellen saw she couldn't talk to him. Trees had always offered refuge, she could see; quite a forest of interesting, nitpicking names. The neck was tanned and slightly gaunt and mangled from the years of supervising in all weathers the plantation's vast design.

"Is something the matter?" he asked.

Among the things she'd been determined to discuss was the idea of dropping everything and making one of their trips to Sydney, to the same hotel standing on the same rounded corner at Bondi. Perhaps then Mr Cave dutifully trudging in the same footsteps as her father, only more so, would get the message.

Her father had paused, *E. sepulcralis* in one hand.

As a way to say, "I'm all right, don't worry", Ellen stretched and kissed his rough skin. And as she did she felt an outflow of weakness; her despair trickled into sadness for him.

If he had turned and looked at her, just then, she would have collapsed into shoulder-shaking and tears. Head bent he began lighting a cigarette. What was happening to her? She felt ill.

It was not long ago as a child she liked to put her feet into her father's huge brogues and stagger around the house.

Now she was the daughter about to go.

To prevent the disaster overflowing she breathed through her mouth. At least her room offered some sort of refuge, soft in its familiarity, as the trees enveloped him.

She made to go and, part of her awkwardness, reached out for a small wooden box on the mantelpiece, a thing she'd never seen before.

"Take it," came his voice, "I found it the other day. It was your mother's. She never got to see it. I was passing a ridiculously expensive junk shop off Oxford Street, man serving was sandpapering a woman's head, and I thought I'd give it to your mother, to cheer her up. It's a brilliant example of Swiss engineering, but . . . anyway, you'll see it wasn't suitable."

He called out, "Use the key on the bit of string."

Ellen carried the antique box on outstretched palms, like a nurse delivering fresh towels, the only object in the house which had a past reaching to her mother.

Back in her room she felt hemmed in on all sides: not by the painted walls, more by her father squatting over every eucalyptus name in the book, and Mr Cave, advancing with his reliable tread. But then she became furious not at them but at the other one, the mostly invisible unreliable one, who fitted her age and interests and everything else, who'd

217

decided after all those stories no longer to appear, not to help – leaving her.

Ellen no longer knew what to do, where to go.

And tears began their rise, from the warm well of them, not far within, a transparency of emotion, of all she was helpless about just then. These tears reached her mouth first. She held them back. She gasped and bit back these tears. So they returned to her eyes, which were already blinking, ready to flood. Almost immediately she opened herself, and felt the unravelling of her solid difficult self, all those confusions, into soft transparency, release in the form of obliviousness. Besides, there was nothing else to do.

Absently she turned the key, winding up the box meant for her mother.

The Dictionary of Miracles has multiple entries on the appearance of extraordinary tears, almost as many as water into wine and talking without a tongue. The weeping mosaics: a long and hypnotic history. Tears imply a purification; sorrow into ecstasy is a religious movement. Jesus wept. Saints are recorded among the serene weepers in history. Their tears go upwards, "by paths unknown to us". Tears otherwise flow to a future, a result. Men and women are invariably attracted to rivers. Tears activate disintegration and impotence; during the disintegration of a weeping woman's face the man experiences a corresponding impotence – impotence of a stranded, impatient kind, impotence of useful speech. Tears themselves flow from the uselessness of words. At the same time, men – to place the subject on the broadest flood plain – expect and want and often imagine a particular woman weeping. Many are the angry and dissatisfied women. By weeping less, if at all, men at least retain the use of words, to convince.

Still more than the recorded miracles of tears, weeping women are honoured in art. These are women on canvas lost in weeping, faces disintegrated into multiple planes, for example, or smooth faces with a single glistening tear, directing our eye, and others suspended on the very edge of – eyes swimming, lips apart, gazing up from reading a letter or staring out of frame from the bridal chamber.

At that moment Ellen was about to slither over to the full release of tears, when the varnished lid of the musical box sprang open, and coming forward on worn joints and up into a vertical position, like a mummy out of a grave, stood a figure of a straw-blonde, which was exactly her mother's hair, only here was a milkmaid with blushing cheeks and a suitable cleavage, holding a porcelain bucket.

Only one of the pine-laden alpine landscapes, Germany, Switzerland, Austria, would have produced, in reaction against the sublime, such a piece of uncertain kitsch.

Indistinct music from a glockenspiel now came from the box.

And as Ellen gazed and held back her own tears the milkmaid began mechanically *weeping into the bucket*. Most certainly there was a story behind this. A passing man had probably taken advantage of her in one of the treeless meadows, as they are called. The milkmaid had since passed through many hands.

Lying on the bed Ellen studied the unhappiness of the pink blonde. Ellen saw she was about her own age. Whenever the flow of tears slowed down Ellen wound it up again. In that way she let the mechanical figure do the weeping.

Weeping Box (*E. patellaris*) shows near creeks or on low slopes in unusually wide-apart locations: in the western part of the Northern Territory, and across to a spot near Port Hedland, in Western Australia. It has grey, fibrous bark; branchlets of pendulous or "weeping" aspect (this applies to many eucalypts). Another smaller one which appears to weep, *E. sepulcralis*, is named after European cemeteries.

32

Ligulata

LITTLE POINT HERE in describing the faulty photography of dreams.

It is true Ellen woke early to find she had had dreams about him. And this immediately gave him a deeper, more insistent presence, as if he had been sharing her bed, the warmth of her own self, certainly more than he realised. To Ellen the dreams made him less of a stranger, yet more of a stranger.

The trouble is, who can be confident on the origins of a dream, and what it may or may not mean?

There are many variables at work here. A dream may represent nothing in particular, the way images or situations in broad daylight have no particular meaning or effect. Not all dreams have significance. Dreams too need to take a rest! Plenty of dreams, perhaps even the majority, are recollections of something arbitrary, a languid replay of something seen that morning, nothing more. The trigger all the way from the unconscious may have no psychological significance at all. The trigger may be as arbitrary as the Tumbledown Gum that happened to be standing in the path of young Sheldrake on the fateful Thursday as he left the dirt road by the river, speeding in his father's red truck (the eucalypt was called *dealbata*).

Ellen, though, she welcomed the privacy of dreams: in them she saw her strange feelings rendered still more strangely. At least she and he could float in a concentrated oneness; Ellen woke warm and wet, in grateful disbelief. These dreams perhaps exaggerated her feelings for him. As soon as she woke she recorded them in her journal.

Beneath a frail specimen of *E. nelsonii* Ellen had quietly listened to almost a story about a Melbourne man blind from birth who regularly dreamed of images such as the sea and musical instruments and a goat repeatedly running underneath a horse, things needless to say he could not possibly have seen. It included a version of his own small face, which was near enough.

Descriptions of dreams have a dubious place in story-telling. For these are dreams which have been imagined – "dreamed up", to be slotted in. A story can be made up. How can a dream be made up? By not rising of its own free will from the unconscious it sets a note of falsity, merely illustrating something "dream-like", which may be why dream descriptions within stories seem curiously meaningless. To avoid glazing over, best then to turn the page quickly.

"Cheer up, girl," her father touched her shoulder. She was pouring the tea from the old brown pot. "It's not the end of the world."

He remained looking at her.

Ellen was still in her dressing gown. Then he did something he hadn't done since she was a girl. Encircling her waist he gently pulled her onto his lap, where she became smothered in his years, his whiskers and tobacco, the fairly firm straightforwardness which showed in the smallness of his movements. "There's a good girl . . . " he kept stroking her hair.

Ellen decided not to object, and not to cry. She swung from one to the other; just managed to hold herself.

Holland merely noticed.

Resting one elbow on the table Ellen stayed on his lap longer than she intended.

Together they heard steps crunching on the gravel drive. At any moment Mr Cave would begin thudding across the wooden verandah. Ellen felt her father sigh.

Mr Cave's voice had been getting louder the closer he was getting to his prize, and a sort of abrupt informality had overrun all his arm and leg movements. Now he was letting himself in through the front door, already part of the family.

"The bridge is down," he reported.

Holland looked up.

"What are you talking about?"

"The one that's been here since the year dot, the little footbridge. The river's gone mad and taken most of it away."

"What a shame," Ellen murmured.

Her father said, "Never used . . . on its last legs . . . one man's obsession . . . "

The home-made bridge had stood as something firm in the midst of all the shimmer and fluidity near the bend in the river, where Ellen had once upon a time gazed down and dangled her feet.

"And this," Mr Cave assumed a mysterious face. "Guess what I find hanging on a Maiden Gum. There's a nail hammered in the tree."

With the forensic flourish employed by stern husbands he held up Ellen's dress, now dried to a delicate shade of pale rhubarb or a long slice of ham (with small blue buttons).

To Holland it made more of an impact than the news of the bridge. He looked perplexed.

"There's wild women in among those trees," Mr Cave grinned. Both men stared at the dress.

Quite suddenly Ellen didn't feel like standing there. And as she remained in the one spot, banging her hip against the table, she became overwhelmed with an elaborate, flowing looseness. All her joints became weak: the bone, blood and tissue. It invaded her eyes and throat; such a weary softness. She even became hard of hearing.

From across the river she heard her father clear his throat; but he was still in the kitchen, putting on his coat to go off with Mr Cave. Ellen could see his puzzled look. She wondered if she had been rude to Mr Cave.

In the empty house Ellen undressed and returned to bed, which is where Holland found her, early in the afternoon. It was so unusual he sat beside her, placing a hand on her forehead, and asking questions, which she scarcely nodded to. At the slightest mention of food she closed her eyes.

The doctor in town was an old bachelor. At all hours he wore a linen jacket, stained with bits of food, and in the manner of rural doctors almost too common to mention he had a worn, distracted expression. It was as if he didn't really belong in the town. At St Vincent's in Sydney he had been resident surgeon and drove a Rover. Something happened either there or in his private life. It was never spoken about, and he never once returned to Sydney. He still had nightmares. Sometimes they could be heard from the footpath, yet next morning making his rounds he had the most careful of smiles. He was courteous, always nodding encouragement. Often he was invited to houses for dinner and, however many glasses he may have had, rolled up his surgeon's sleeves and carved the roast with a precision that never failed to leave the table spellbound.

Seated now on Ellen's bed, he talked about this and that. He took her temperature and asked her to poke out her tongue.

When he first arrived in town, he said, it was very much as it was today. After the war there were two or three extra widows, that was all. One of them, Mrs Jessie Cork, had a dream. It was about the house he was having built. She came to the hotel early one morning in her dressing gown and banged on his door. In her dream Jessie Cork saw he should move the house. It was luckier on the other side of the hill, which is why she had come straight around to tell him. "This can be the trouble with dreams," the doctor said to Ellen. Adding, "Have you been getting a proper night's sleep?" One of the first things a doctor learns is to bite his tongue, he said. After a brief delay the house was finished. Not long after, when he was called out on an emergency, there was a fire at the place and the house with all his belongings burned to the ground.

If she wasn't any better, the doctor said to Holland, he'd return in the morning.

Since there was nothing in particular the matter with her, Ellen decided to remain in bed.

33

Abbreviata

THIS RECENT REPORT from Santiago under the heading, NO SECOND CHANCE:

> A Chilean policeman who escaped death last year when a robber's bullet ricocheted off a pen in his breast pocket died when a tree fell on his squad car. Hector Zapata Cuevas was crushed when a giant eucalyptus crashed onto the car during a storm. – Reuters

On the other hand, he mentioned in passing, eucalypts have made plenty of contributions to the progress and well-being of the human race. Overall the influence of the eucalypt has been positive. Aside from the many railway sleepers opening up drowsy continents, and telegraph poles (*E. diversicolor*) which have played their part in transmitting urgent business as well as intimate personal messages, there is quite a catalogue of wagon axles fashioned from ironbark, piles cut for bridges and jetties which are still standing, and for grey shearing sheds (which have produced the wool which has produced the clothing which has . . .), along with pulpits for delivering His Word throughout the New World – hard on the heels of the demand for billiard tables; sideboards too of Jarrah, believe it or not, for holding the numbing qualities of Australian sherry and brandy, the same-grained timber chosen for hundreds of piano lids – and the varieties of pleasure they must have encouraged; sturdy carved legs and bedheads have supported the mattresses and pillows and whispered words for the procreation of tribes of imaginative, tolerant humans – of course those legs could tell a few secrets, he had smiled. Whole forests of Jarrah from Western Australia have been tongue-and-grooved into ballroom dancing floors all over the place, so many stories there with a beginning, a middle and end; other forests continue to be consumed for fine-paper making (for printing works of an artistic, philosophical or medical nature); flagpoles and crutches have been made from straight-grained eucalypts; honey comes from these trees; a Mr Ramel in Victoria gave the men in Havana a fright in the 1860s by patenting *eucalyptus cigars* made from the leaves of gum trees; speaking of patents still pending there are the various eucalyptus oils in their authoritative bottles and jars which claim – it's there in black-and-white – to cure or ease a remarkable number of serious ailments, everything from the common cold to – .

34

Illaguens

DAY AFTER DAY Ellen lay gradually fading.

Lying exceptionally still, she emptied herself of every pictorial thought, especially of the near future, and began to float in a drift of pure helplessness, the pillows and cotton sheets as soft as clouds. Then a crow outside would break into its harsh lament, a sound she had grown up alongside, accordingly grown deaf to, though here nagging her in the coarsest way imaginable about her precise position on a dry part of the earth.

In this way Ellen lost track of time, of whole days.

As though she were already dead, Mr Cave crept about and spoke in loud whispers, holding his hat in both hands, as it were. Out of respect and bewilderment in general he slowed down to a crawl the naming of the last remaining trees. Holland anyway could spare only an hour or two with him, not wanting to leave his one and only daughter. Never had Ellen looked so pale; a pale speckled beauty, indenting the pillows.

For all her hopes of drift Ellen kept returning to him, and the way he spoke, how easily she had wandered with him, one eucalypt to the next.

"These trees," he had remarked early on, "could be fitted with nameplates the way they do it in zoos and the Botanical Gardens. Easy to read at two paces! Can withstand all weathers!" He stood before a slender Spinning Gum (*E. perriniana*) in direct line with the Salmon Gum near the front gate. "What do you think?"

"That's making something serious out of something that isn't necessarily," Ellen had said, too hastily.

Now in her room she followed the broad movement of daylight beginning along the ceiling, angling down the blue walls and across the floor where it left her shoes behind dark and misshapen, and late afternoon climbing most of the papered wall, until it dissolved, and all faded grey. Even there, in her room, a eucalypt intruded: through the windows which opened onto the verandah, a shimmer of Fuchsia Gum leaves patterned her sheets into lace and shivered the brushes and little jars and bowls on her dressing table.

The way the stories began in a timeworn way had relaxed her. It was his way. "There was an old woman who lived at the foot of a dark mountain . . . " "The quality of miracles has declined over the years . . . " "Late in the evening of the 11th . . . " "There was once a man who . . . " These old arrangements of words caused Ellen to smile secretly and return to the trees, at which point she grew thoughtful and began to frown – another version of day replaced by evening and night.

Remaining motionless Ellen tried to decipher a shape to the stories; she even followed the contours of the plantation, somehow taking an aerial view of the stories, as if that would reveal a hidden pattern.

Many were about daughters; or women almost requiring a man for themselves. A woman finds a man and something unfortunate happens. It doesn't last. There were certainly more stories about women than men, she could see. It wasn't necessary to count them up. A daughter can never become a separate woman, not really. Fathers had strong and impassive positions in the world of stories, too. Many of his stories concerned a father, or how he'd clean forgotten his daughter, thereby introducing a note of real sadness. Why had he been telling her this? The women seemed to be searching or waiting for something else, something almost indefinable but extra nevertheless, such as a solution somewhere else or with someone, she at once saw and recognised. These were women who followed the idea of hope. It seemed to be their *greatest obedience*. Ellen couldn't help respecting them. These women, one by one, moved about with a form of lightness, and obeyed their ideas of truth to feelings. Ellen usually liked the women he happened to talk about. Under the Spinning Gum he had his hands in his pockets as he turned to face her. "Off the coast of Victoria," he shielded his eyes, "was a wife of a lighthouse keeper who became addicted to kite flying. She was young and had no children. For weeks at a time she saw nobody else. Supplies such as flour, tea and sugar were hauled up to the lighthouse window in a wicker basket, from a small dark boat. Her husband was a much older man who could go for weeks on end without saying a word. She flew the kite from the rocks at the base of the lighthouse, where she was happiest. One day her husband looked down and shouted at her and she got such a fright she let go of the kite, which was in the shape of a woman's unhappy face. It flew up into the sky and became entangled in the mast of a passing ship. The captain was a young man with a fresh beard. It was his first command . . .

"What is it you are laughing at?" He too began to laugh, the day he placed his hand on her hip.

As Ellen faded she became frail at the edges, at times curiously elongated, a mile long, and still in her bed she gathered the stories which naturally included him from different angles. He made no reference to general knowledge, except to say on one occasion it was "probably overrated". It was little more than a good memory, as he put it.

And yet to tell the stories it was necessary for him to know the names of many eucalypts; only by lying still in bed did Ellen realise. The Victoria Spring Mallee had forced a bulge in the southern fence; *E. prominens*, according to him. "A small town – I forget where, exactly – known for its wild rose honey and its small women with dark eyebrows, where the keyholes to the houses are shaped as hearts . . . " Story followed story, in and out of the trees – these unpleasant, unhelpful trees. In Sparkle Street in Blacktown (the local mayors in Sydney's outer suburbs often like to give demonstrations of their skills in nomenclature) a man tattooed his three daughters. One he had tattooed with a thistle, another a rose, and the eldest, a small telephone . . . *E. melanoleuca*. Elsewhere, there was the travelling salesman who became a wholesaler of eggs, married to the skinny shrew of a wife who bore him nothing but freckled children, and broke plates during the slightest disagreement.

It was not always necessary to tell a story, although Ellen preferred them. On account of its thickish leaves the Grey Gum of southern Queensland is called Leather Jacket. This was enough for him to say the bikies who sit astride their heavy machines are the modern, necessary equivalent to medieval knights on horseback. Bikies too stagger under the weight of protective gear, the helmet and visor, their boots resting on stirrups. The machines they handle and acceler- ate away in small groups are powerful, draped in leather and chains; a large motorbike is a version of a sturdy horse in all its power and heat underneath. At this point Ellen could have asked about the small snick below his eye, the History of a Scar; there was a story written there: but he had already moved on to the next tree.

So restful, so vague, sifting through like this. It was at a half-conscious level, just below the brighter waking surface; paddling in the shallows of her private river, as it were.

At intervals her father and others came into her room, casting shadows. She was almost grateful to have his rough hand around hers. The roughness of his hand made her feel softer still. Her hand felt like a small bird held in his.

At mid-morning, Mr Cave's voice broke through louder than usual, announcing victory. Apparently he wanted to come straight into her room to celebrate. What would he have done then?

Ellen closed her eyes, and turned to the wall.

35

Rameliana

IN THE EARLY 1920s a young Frenchman from Lyons was sent by his father-in-law on a business trip to Australia. He left behind a young wife and their daughter barely six months old.

The prospect appeared before him as a long and rare adventure. The undulating shape of Australia in the blue of the southern ocean beckoned in all its mysterious emptiness. He had never met anyone who'd actually been there. Cuba and Tahiti, yes, but not Australia. The closest was a Russian emigré tennis coach he'd met socially who claimed to have seen the gigantic straw-coloured outline fluctuating before him during a recent heart attack.

And now here he was about to go there himself!

In many respects he was an ideal choice. He was thin, dark-eyed, with restless fingers. He had so much curiosity he was something of a dreamer; and like many Frenchmen he had a surprising affinity for *déserts*, the purity of emptiness, and so on, which he expressed in transports of volubility faintly embarrassing to his father-in-law. For all the Sahara-looking emptiness, and its rather thin population, Australia has, as we now know, considerable treecover, plenty of shade, what with all those eucalypts wherever you look, as well as acacias, even in what are called deserts. Not knowing what to expect he included in his luggage a water bottle and crystals for purifying water.

As he farewelled his wife, who wept while waving the loose hand of their yawning daughter, his father-in-law repeated last-minute instructions.

He was to photograph Aboriginals in their natural state, focusing in particular on their cuisine, and the initiation and marriage ceremonies, which apparently hark back to the Stone Age, and while he was at it collect as many of their myths and legends as possible. The father-in-law was planning an ethnographical museum on the outskirts of Paris, where the various myths told by the Aboriginal people could be put into some sort of order, alongside images of their daily lives, all under the one roof.

The voyage was smooth and the young Frenchman stepped ashore at Brisbane. Soon after he set out for the interior.

His letters to his wife spoke of a toothache and his loneliness, and the difficulty of actually finding any natives living as in the Stone Age. He expressed love for her in ways appropriate to a young Frenchman, and scribbled little messages to their daughter, although of course she was too young to read, let alone write. For his father-in-law he neatly transcribed a few myths and legends he'd heard, including one about how the crow became black (it had originally been white), and offered some tentative jottings for an Aboriginal dictionary.

After about six months the first group of photographic

plates arrived: the further he travelled from the coast the fewer items of clothing the Aboriginals wore – but because they still had on skirts and trousers they were not much use for the museum. In subsequent photographs these were replaced by views of stony outcrops and gorges, all sharply shadowed, tracks petering out to nowhere, creekbeds with dark birds, a cliff split asunder by the white trunk of a eucalypt; and the next batch shifted still further to one-horse towns, good-natured barmaids, and filthy bore-diggers south of Darwin drinking tea from dented mugs. Although there was nothing like this in all of France the father-in-law felt compelled to remind his agent of the mission, upon which the hopes of the proposed museum depended.

While the Frenchman's wife waited and slowly became more silent the daughter grew tall into her teens; sometimes she would study her face in the mirror for possible signs of her far-distant father.

As for the wife, she feared he would no longer recognise her when he returned.

In less than a year he had stopped sending photographs. He explained he was moving about in difficult country, "extended wilderness of sand and hardwood", as he put it. Over long periods there were no letters at all. The letters that did arrive to his wife were on grubby paper, written in blunt pencil. Both she and her father wondered what was going on. He seemed to have been swallowed by the desert.

Then at last – after more than fifteen years had passed – he wrote to say he was returning home. He had sent his luggage ahead, saying he would follow.

There was much relief and excitement in France. The now elderly father-in-law was on hand to supervise the unpacking of the trunks. There was the camera, its tripod and cape. Grimly he noticed the boxes of unused photographic plates. From other trunks he unwrapped a few boomerangs, as well as an authentic woomera and a bark painting. There was personal clothing, and a pipe, which his wife took into their bedroom. There was a bow tie and a shaving mug. Some books. A fine coating of red dust over everything, which left little pyramids on the carpet, suggested they had been a long time in storage.

As the wife waited for him to make his appearance she suffered a series of small illnesses, like the aftershocks of a strong earthquake. Fifteen years of waiting had been hard; she had lived more the life of a widow than a wife. And now he would be returning as a different man; even his skin would not have the smoothness she remembered. She kept returning to their marriage photograph to check his appearance. And she constantly examined herself in the mirror and tried on shoes and old dresses.

The daughter too was interested in her father's return. She was doing well at school. To her, he was a stranger, simultaneously close yet distant, with precious little form or shape; a ghost.

In their different ways they waited.

Again months passed, and more.

Years later when she was finely wrinkled (as if someone had draped a net over her face) and her daughter had moved to a job in Brussels, she discovered her young husband had died at a place near Cloncurry – and also that she was very rich.

He had wandered off the beaten path; moved away from his original aims.

In Australia he was constantly embarrassed. In his travels into the interior, then back to the coast and the cities, he encountered people who were invariably *types*, difficult types, insistent types.

He went everywhere with a dictionary in his pocket. So many strangers welcomed him into their shacks and tents with open arms.

In Sydney at a boarding house for men, near the harbour, he met a bearded man who made a powerful impression. Here was a man who had committed a mistake, something about a daughter – refused to give details – and could no longer look himself in the face. For more than thirty years he had successfully avoided all mirrors. He stayed mostly indoors, and even refused to see his daughter in case he saw something of himself in her. Needless to say, he could no longer be sure of what he now looked like. While his clothes were exceptionally neat his face was a congestion of lines which moved like the spokes of an umbrella when he talked. Whatever the merits in what he was attempting it had a degree of philosophical difficulty that demanded respect.

The more the young Frenchman was diverted from his mission on behalf of the ethnographical museum the more flimsy did his presence seem. He had no difficulty in seeing the shadows of photography as a form of chemical theft.

The actual earth, the flora and fauna, simply had more substance.

What happened to him became legend itself. In his second year, alone in the backblocks of western Queensland, he happened to stub his foot on a jutting rock. The rock glittered, and when he found others he said something aloud in French. He could not believe what he saw. On the site now is an enormous silver mine, illuminated at night, working around the clock every day. Such accidental discoveries were still possible then in the New World.

His unexpected death a few days before returning to France was just as casual, accidental too.

All along his widow had lived with her own precious silver deposit, a photograph, smaller than her hand, of him standing beside her larger father in serge; it was then he moved from the tree and turned to Ellen, shielding his eyes, she now remembered.

36

Baileyana

ALTHOUGH SHE WANDERED over the many different surfaces of her room, where her eyes had rested many times before, Ellen never tired of it. All was muted and soft, a comfort. The air of worn familiarity offered important soothing qualities, it seemed.

Yet Ellen tossed and slid about throughout light and dark, from one end of herself to its opposite.

She was both calm and agitated; suffered extended lassitude; in the next breath, restlessness. There has to be a stout medical term for this up and down and contradictory sliding-across condition.

Although she lay in bed she remained unrested. Although she welcomed the sun and its warmth, as well as the many faint sounds of the outside world, she would suddenly from her pillows picture a tree, and feel a hatred of trees, of all her father's trees. She never wanted to see another sprig of drooping khaki leaves ever again. She could no longer face the world. How could she go on living on the property?

In this mood Ellen went back over her clothes, tried on her shoes. She went back to the almost bare shops in Sydney, where the thin women in black had served with their noses tilted. Then she had a sudden mad impulse to give all her good clothes away, including the cream dress with white buttons and her red shoes. At night she woke up talking or at least with her mouth wide open, while during the day she remained in bed with scarcely a word. Her temperature rose, she went into decline. It was simply beyond her strength to halt the decline, which sometimes imitated a physical movement, such as slowly sliding off the end of the bed, into nothing; nor, at that stage, did she care.

A man drowning in a bucket was a terrible dream she had (and what could that possibly represent?).

Until her illness, her father out of some unspoken tact had never entered her room; and now he was sitting at the end of the bed for hours at a stretch, or else popping his head around the door to see if she was all right.

Some afternoons she opened her eyes to find several men seated beside her bed, watching her.

The old doctor in his linen jacket was a regular; Ellen saw how his face, marbled by the morning light, looked unhappily out of time and place. Reading her temperature, and asking the same questions, he tapped a fingernail on his teeth. He sat there a good hour or more. Ellen liked it when he began humming.

Ha! To cheer her up her father enquired in his finest wheedling voice, "I don't suppose a man is allowed to have a smoke?" And by the time she could begin to nod, let alone imply a memory-laden smile, the match had flared – there's a deeply geological sound.

Meanwhile, Mr Cave moved in with his brown suitcase, hat and hairbrushes to one of the spare rooms. He was in the house all day, clearing his throat. Part of the family, more or less, he felt comfortable with his rights. He was patient.

Still, he was beginning to wonder if this drama had anything to do with him. After all, the naming of more than five hundred trees was not as easy as it looked. (Dozens had been spirited away from the most obscure corners of Australia.) And as the number of successfully ticked-off names accumulated, the dark cluster of shifting-about names took on an almighty weight and height, like a library about to keel over. He could feel it himself. Once past the halfway mark the greater would be his public fall! Ellen's future too depended on his success or failure; she would have been on edge, obviously. It could have affected her health.

On the last day he had stumbled. As he made his way with Holland up the gravel drive, naming each tree, left and right, a monarch counting up his loyal subjects, he saw ahead the front door, which represented victory with all its associations of ownership, warmth and entry: perhaps that was it. For Mr Cave wandered. He had a hybrid stringybark in his mouth and on the tip of his tongue, but did a double-take on the leaves – to this day he doesn't know why – and correctly switched to the tree known for its fifteen different vernacular names, *E. dealbata*. Holland saw how close he had come to falling.

In the kitchen munching on a biscuit Mr Cave asked if Ellen's illness could possibly be related to him. Holland spoke sharply, "I don't think so. Nothing is one."

So Mr Cave waited, anxious to help. Knocking on her door, for example, and bringing in tea on a tray could be seen as an example of his good intentions.

* *

It is not normal for a body to remain horizontal; beyond a certain length of time it attracts concern. Death and burial ("laid to rest") are seen as the natural horizontal states, which is surely why the calculated falsity of perpendicular deaths, such as hangings, crucifixions, burnings at the stake, etc. produce such indelible shock.

News of Ellen's continuing horizontality had a procession of concerned citizens calling and depositing home-made jams, boiled fruitcakes and flowers, and plenty of home-spun advice. Few of them had been inside the dark homestead before.

Every morning the doctor arrived, but still he couldn't give a name to the illness.

The Sprunt sisters took the opportunity of looking around Ellen's room, and taking in the darkened lounge room, and the butcher's wife began bossing Holland about in the kitchen, until he told her to clear out. Otherwise Holland didn't know what to do. The postmistress sent a steady stream of cards, while Mrs Brain from the hotel dropped in two bottles of Adelaide stout. Someone else left a new calendar – another Ghost Gum, with sheep and the usual slack fencing.

In the town the only question asked of Holland concerned his daughter. Women admired Ellen; no difficulty there. They wanted her back on her feet. To have such a beauty in the district somehow reflected favourably on them.

To Mr Cave a woman lying in bed during daylight represented a complete mass of confusion and mystery.

Sometimes he and Holland sat by the bed together.

Ellen showed no inclination to talk, turning slightly away when Mr Cave came forward with some extra-special eucalyptus oil, said to cure everything under the sun.

All Mr Cave could offer was patience, which is a variety of kindness.

One morning a pause stretched into an awkward two hours or more, no sign of Holland, so Mr Cave idly picked up the weeping milkmaid from the bedside table. He nodded thoughtfully, "Made in good old Austria . . . "

With blunt persistent fingers he tried turning the key. "Don't . . . " Ellen whispered.

There was a loud snapping sound: this man had broken the wind-up mechanism. And Ellen wept.

From then on Ellen's decline became steeper. No one could do anything. She herself was a ribbon floating down from a height to the earth where it would rest, possibly forever. In her weakness Ellen felt a dangerous contentment.

She was losing her beauty.

The doctor now wondered whether to call in a distinguished colleague, unless he had migrated to America.

The butcher's wife returned this time with other women and, with Mr Cave looking on, urged Holland to send the patient straightaway to Sydney. At this Ellen shook her head almost violently, and closed her eyes.

It was one of those illnesses without a name. She could only be brought back to life by a story.

37

Approximans

A CHAIR WAS placed beside the bed for men to sit and tell their stories.

The advantage of this was that from the story-teller's chair they could roam with their eyes unhindered all over Ellen's speckled face, which in normal circumstances reduced the strongest men to mumblers and shufflers.

Too old to do much about feminine beauty the doctor began by telling Ellen about some of his more curious surgical cases. It was as though he was talking to himself, not really addressing her, and Ellen too drifted off. After he left, Ellen almost fell to the floor as she went to close the French windows. Normally before returning to bed she would look at herself in the mirror, perhaps run a brush through her hair; but she went straight back and faced the wall.

The young locals no doubt at the insistence of their mothers sat in the chair and rattled off anecdotes about pig-shooting, and snakes of impossible length and ferocity they'd come across. Exaggerations, they have a useful part in the telling process. At least Trevor Traill launched into the adventures of his great-uncle, born so far inland he joined the merchant navy the day he turned sixteen, and went around the world. The family congregated when he returned. The first thing he did on staggering ashore, according to family legend, was to go down on his knees and *kiss a pig*.

It was the same with the very decent schoolteacher. He came in on tiptoe and read to her from a British history book, and when asked if she wanted more of the same tomorrow she appeared to shake her head.

Mr Cave had observed how Ellen stirred the moment a man sat in the chair and began a story; by her posture he could tell she was listening. He too would have to try something. If a story he told could bring her back to life their problems, whatever they were, were solved. He began racking his brains. It's always easier telling a story in the first person. The going feels altogether smoother. It can produce a rushing frankness in the story-teller, as if the "I" was actually revealing some distinct inner truth.

Mr Cave took his place late one morning. He seemed to gather his thoughts, then he shifted on the seat.

"I have a story. It concerns my fiancée."

Ellen stirred. Pleats and creases (out of the corner of her eye), and still not a hair out of place, combined to make his words unusually direct.

"I very nearly got married. This was some time back, in Adelaide. Her name was Marjorie.

"Small mouth, wiry hair. She had a thing about cashmere sweaters, I don't know why. Always asking me to get one whenever I went interstate. Father, a public servant. Department of Higher Education, if I'm not mistaken. It was some years back. Marjorie used to poke fun at my eucalyptic studies, and was always telling me to grow a moustache." Mr Cave let out a laugh. "She could get on her high horse! Chose to differ with her on a matter, forget what, and she clocked me one.

"Otherwise we got on all right. For several years we saw each other a few times a week.

"One day she said the following: 'I'm almost forty, I like being with you. But my family think I should be married. Let me know on Tuesday. Otherwise I'll have to find someone else.'

"Words to that effect.

"So there I was. On the Tuesday in question we had arranged to have a meal in the evening. Chinese, if my memory serves, in Hindley Street. We talked about this and that. Mostly I talked. She had her eye on the clock, couldn't sit still for a second. At one stage I thought she would rush out of the room. I waited until a few seconds before midnight before giving the answer. She was relieved, then for some reason she was angry at me. Next minute she started to work out the invitations and so on.

"I remember thinking her face had softened. Quite beautiful, I felt like saying."

Ellen had turned from the wall.

"This funny thing happened." Mr Cave had his arms folded. "Seemed simple enough at the time. A chap at the office put me onto this. Marjorie and I were seeing each other every day now. A lot of business to get through. I took her into a pawnshop, where they had a jar full of wedding rings."

The story had been going smoothly enough, with suitable pauses. Ellen had her eyes open to the ceiling.

Mr Cave coughed. "Marjorie had her hand in the jar, bringing out rings, as if they were toffees. All looked the same to me. She apparently knew what she wanted. She had her hand still in the jar when she stopped, and seemed to be thinking. 'No!' She suddenly pushed it away, '*I want eighteen carats!*' I didn't know what she was talking about. Then she bolted, left me standing in the shop, half a dozen wedding rings in my hands. Some years back."

Ellen had her mouth open, not looking at him.

"That," Mr Cave rubbed his hands, "is about the only story I can think of that's happened to me."

Holland who had listened to the end managed a laugh, "*Eighteen carats*? Why not twenty-four?"

He noticed Ellen had turned to the wall and was very still.

"I think she could do with a rest," Holland winced. "You'd better go."

38

Crebra

T HE NARROW LEAF Red Ironbark: now there's an employment of no-nonsense *nouniness*. This eucalypt has a straight trunk and hard, deeply furrowed bark, like a strip of dark grey clay dried out after being ploughed. The leaves are noticeably narrow. What isn't described is their "weeping habit" (a technical term); that is, leaves drooping in a shimmer of real melancholy.

This suspended air of perpetual sadness would be of little consequence, except the Narrow Leaf Red Ironbark is one of the most common eucalypts on earth; certainly they crowd the woodland areas of eastern Australia, all the way up to the top of Queensland. The botanical name recognised this in the very beginning: *crebra* from the Latin "frequent", "in close succession".

Imagine the effect of such widespread statements of melancholy on the common mood. Needless to say it has permeated and reappeared in the long faces of our people, where the jaw has lengthened, and in words formed by almost imperceptible mouth movements, which often filter the mention of excessive emotions. It has shaded in khaki-grey our everyday stories, and when and how they are told, even the myths and legends, such as they are, just as surely as the Norwegians have been formed by snow and ice.

The eucalypts may be seen as daily reminders of the sadnesses between fathers and daughters, the deadpan stoicism of nature (which of course isn't stoicism at all), drought and melting asphalt in the cities. Each leaf hanging downwards suggests another hard-luck story or a dry line or joke to wave away the flies.

Only a small number of other eucalypts, those pale and stately beauties that have achieved fame on tea towels, postage stamps and calendars, correct the general impression of melancholy, as put forward by *E. crebra* and some of the other ironbarks. They bring a glow of light to a paddock, a rockface, a footpath in the city: the two Salmon Gums standing in the traffic island between the university and the cemetery in Melbourne! It only needs a few. Theirs is a majestic statement on what is alive and spreading: continuation.

And there is a parallel nearby. It may not be exaggeration to say that the formidable instinct in men to measure, which is often mistaken for pessimism, is counterbalanced by the unfolding optimism of women, which is nothing less than life itself; their endless trump card.

It is shown in miniature by the reverence women have for flowers, at its most concentrated when they look up and in recognition of their natural affinity accept flowers.

39

Confluens

O N   T H E   S E V E N T E E N T H   day Ellen still lay in her
room. No one had told a story to bring her back to life.

If anything Mr Cave's story only made matters worse.

As far as he was concerned he had won Ellen's hand
according to the rules, the father looking over his shoulder
every inch of the way. By any standard it was an impressive
feat of memory and perseverance, a test so difficult Holland
had not imagined any man passing it. If Mr Cave was to set
out and do it all over again he might well fall by the
wayside. And now at the entirely unexpected outcome he
was too baffled and sincere to protest.

"Making myself scarce," he said in Ellen's hearing,
Mr Cave wandered out to be where he felt most comfortable, among what he knew about more than anything –
eucalypts, in all their truly remarkable variety.

For the moment there was little Holland could do. He
was left contemplating his knuckles, which had never held
much interest, and now appeared larger than normal. It was
enough to provoke a grim laugh, one which shot up his
shoulders, and for Ellen to wonder what in her situation
could be so funny.

It was a matter of waiting. Time as always held the answers, was Holland's opinion. All things are processed by time. That was about all he could say to Mr Cave, a man he had grown to like, or at least respect. But at the first word, "Time . . . ", he let it go.

There were things he wanted to say to Ellen. But they were obscure and difficult; and he was different from his daughter.

Ellen liked it when he took his place in the chair. At night his cigarette glowed in the dark as parts of the house creaked back to a lower set of temperatures, and he went over again in a vague circular murmur the sad story of her mother, for she too had faded away in a gradual seepage of paleness.

The more Ellen listened the less she understood her father . . . She knew him better than anyone else, she realised, yet she didn't really know him at all. Although she hardly knew the stranger – and there was every reason to connect "strange" to him – Ellen realised she knew him better than her own father.

At this revelation she lay with her eyes open, and mixed up with it was a clear view of the man from different angles, near trees. And all the time she concentrated on the cigarette glow in the dark, although it too began to fade. When it completely faded the man was gone – from the property, from being near her. All along it had been ridiculous, and she began blinking in fury.

Still she kept seeing his face and hearing the voice although she wanted perhaps to banish him. She didn't expect ever to see him again. She didn't feel like seeing anyone.

Pale and distant Ellen receded further into the depths of the sheets and pillows, and her beauty spots and their narcotic history of imprinting into the minds of men and fumbling their tongues – these legendary spots now came forward and seemed out of harmony with the rest of her face, and even other parts, such as her throat and tapering hands, as if the spots were too many and too dark.

The women from town and the surrounding properties could see the father was doing everything wrong; he didn't know what was going on. And he was taking too much notice of their doctor who could only think of liquids. But if anyone whispered that it was high time Ellen was moved to the nearest half-decent town, or over the mountains to Sydney, Ellen facing the wall firmly shook her head, "*I am not . . .*"

It was the most unusual illness Holland had seen in his daughter; it was hardly an illness at all. She hadn't vomited once, for example. If it was a sickness it was some sort of sleeping or semi-speechless sickness. Day after day she was more or less motionless, and spoke only a few words. It was all very well letting people in to sit down and try telling stories. He'd listened to a few himself, and when he turned and saw his daughter had fallen asleep he smiled; such a disappointed, severe sort of sleep.

Holland opened Ellen's room on to the verandah.

For a while he stood there; he normally looked at Ellen and spoke.

Halfway towards the first paddock was a familiar tree: with its weeping habit, its melancholy shiver of leaves on the droop, its cladding of *callous* ironbark, it always seemed resigned to waiting for the worst – for it to be all over – like a hyena in Africa.

When Ellen raised her head to look at her father she too became caught in the tree's gaze.

"Feeling better?" he turned. "Good" – before she could answer.

Now he made an exaggerated search in the pockets of the old dark coat for matches, which Ellen wanted to say were already in one hand.

"Mr Cave's still here, you know," he said at last. "As he sees it, there's no reason for him to go, none whatever. He's a very patient fellow, a methodical one." Her father blew out smoke. "If we had any spare cash we could put him on as gardener. He sure does know his way around the eucalyptus world."

Any other time Ellen might have laughed.

"He can't stand around twiddling his thumbs forever," he added.

In the silence that followed, Holland felt the approach of something, a slowing down and a coming together: almost enough to brush the general awkwardness aside. The small sky-blue room, his daughter's world, existed in equilibrium with the park-like arrangement of trees and the swaying mat-coloured grass outside. Ellen almost felt it too. Whatever it was may have flowed slowly from her. If nothing else the uncertain idea she had of herself had diminished, her resistance gone: water spreading in all directions onto a flood plain. It was not possible to spend the rest of her life in bed, not her best years.

Later when her father came with tea on a tray and went to close the verandah doors Ellen spoke, "I'll see Mr Cave first thing in the morning, tell him."

She turned to the wall and held both warm breasts in her hands. So finally amazed was she at her immovable father she couldn't imagine talking to him – what to say? In his old coat he looked thinner, she had noticed, which only illustrated his stubbornness. Then she began to feel sorry for him, her father, sorry for his stubbornness, which was how she closed her eyes in the dark.

"Now, you might be wondering . . . "
Ellen thought she was dreaming.

If she opened her eyes the voice would go away.

His voice had come in from nothing, no warning, no "Good evening" or anything.

"Are you asleep?"

She had her eyes open, still facing the wall. The voice was very close. Now she was aware of every familiar scrape and blur.

To think that he could just stroll in! The surprise was physical, a surge. Where had he been? Why? He shouldn't come near her at all. In the middle of the night he was in the room.

He had let himself in from the verandah.

She wanted him to go, she wanted him to stay.

On the verge of saying it, and sending him away, she shifted a little, but didn't turn.

"Why are you here?"

Although it was dark the angles of the room converged

towards him, and he displayed impressive sangfroid, the first requirement for Officer Material.

"I am going to switch on the lamp," said Ellen.

If he was found smiling she would ask him to leave. But she had never before seen him away from sunlight and a tree, in her room.

All this was forgotten anyway when the light showed him in an old leather jacket, and accordingly pale, and holding for her a miserable bunch of yellow buds from one of the trees. These demonstrated only too clearly how the eucalypt was named: the reproductive organs "well covered".

"They're nice," said Ellen. "They're beautiful."

It hardly mattered that they were taken from the pessimistic tree a short distance away, *E. crebra*. In her hand as flowers they became one with her, flowing both in and outwards; Ellen felt a firmness within warmth, her rounded warmth faintly functional.

As he watched a mysterious superiority stole over this woman sitting up in bed, before subsiding: a brief reminder.

Passing a hand across her face Ellen wondered about her appearance.

"What a wreck," she said, and slid beneath the blankets, covering herself again.

Now that he was back and actually in her room – his head above and bent towards her – she settled to hear his voice; but almost immediately Ellen met a thinning stain of hopelessness, a reminder of her position, her patient father and Mr Cave waiting in the other rooms. Tomorrow morning wasn't far away; and it was the end.

"I have something to tell you."

First, the flowers; and now one of his stories – as if anything he said could solve anything. Ellen made a slight turn towards the wall. What could he say? He hadn't done enough. Mr Cave had done more, much more. According to her father, he had done all that was required. In his own way Mr Cave was a remarkable fellow, her father had said. It was too late.

"Move over," he whispered.

Ignoring the story-teller's chair which had been placed beside the bed precisely for that purpose he took off his boots, and stretched out beside her.

"There's no point . . . " Ellen spoke slowly.

For a moment he contemplated a spot on the opposite wall. When her father did this it was as if looking for a place to nail up one of his agricultural calendars.

"The most important events of my life," he began, "have taken place in parks, gardens, light forests . . . "

The stories he had told over different parts of the property Ellen all along had assumed were dreamed up on the spot for her benefit, which accounted for her curious possessive interest as she had listened. None of them relied on the usual "I this, I that" which all adds up to "I am". And now, when it was necessary to tell the story of all stories, a story specifically to save her – somehow – for how was that possible now? – he was launching into personal reminiscence, just like everybody else. It wasn't going to save her. Obviously he had no idea of her position.

On the other hand, it might begin to answer some of the many questions about him she'd been wanting to ask.

It also allowed her from the pillow and the warmth of her bed to survey his face from an angle, his jaw moving as he carefully chose his words, which was the way her father absently chewed a steak, especially lately. She suddenly wanted to twist his nose, or at least his ear. Pleasant lines had established around his eyes and mouth. His jaw was almost too strong, as if it had been broken.

As it happened he too felt the disadvantage of having himself at the centre of the narrative and, allowing the opening line to remain as an explanatory remark or a clue, continued without the insistent "I", and spoke quite comfortably about a man who grew up with a difficult step-father, because his mother who rode horses for ribbons ran off with another man, an American engineer, whose speciality was damming rivers in south-east Asia, although Ellen could see it was really about him, his story, and so offered some sort of hope.

This stepfather had a limp from a riding accident. In fact, the leg was as crooked as a young gum tree. It didn't stop him swimming right through winter, which is why he chose to live in a humid block of flats behind Bondi.

He was an unhappy man, slightly deaf, and would turn on the boy, knocking him about, while they lived by the sea – a stepfather in black, very clear watery eyes, in need of a crutch or a stick, he's right out of a fable, the stranger went on to say, beside her.

So the boy grew up among sudden arm movements and shouting, and always there the white light of Bondi. No wonder he turned to botany, quiet, orderly, green; geology would have been quieter still, solid and stationary.

One night a woman moved in with his stepfather; and he was told he could no longer stay. He didn't wait for morning. And soon after he dropped out of his studies.

He was away from Sydney for so long his friends thought he was dead. Several times he himself wondered if he was alive. Beginning in the easy countries above the equator he ended up in difficult countries below the equator. Many things he saw for the first time, and would never see again. So many things happened to him that wouldn't have otherwise happened. It was as he had hoped; he was asking for experience. He saw it as giving *texture*. But it was too deliberate. Yes, there was no doubt about that. Travelling in trains: now there's a life subdivided horizontally into a fleeting length of intervals, marked as it happens by Grey Ironbark or Tallowwood, axed from northern New South Wales. Twice he became lost in forests, in Borneo, somewhere in Poland. He saw an elephant give birth. That was in a teak forest. At Kew Gardens he pushed a wheelbarrow. Did you know there are only two eucalypts at Kew? There was also the sympathetic wife of the world's authority on orchids, the scarf around her head.

At this the man beside her frowned before looking down, "This man's had a rich and varied life . . . "

It was not Ellen's idea of experience; she was not interested in experience, as such. As always though the steady rise and fall of his voice became soothing and she concentrated on that.

After x-number of years he returned to Sydney.

On the second day on a visit to Bondi he saved a man

from drowning, he said. The rescuer himself got into difficulties. On the beach he lay exhausted beside the saved man who was covered in seaweed and blue in the face. A small crowd had gathered.

Listening carefully Ellen pictured the beach she knew well; none of this was going to save her.

Mr Lonsdale, who had been rescued, was a quiet man, the stranger went on. "No, I shouldn't have been out there . . ." he said, coughing up sea water. He was in his late sixties and still wearing his watch. "I don't want to be a nuisance."

Mr Lonsdale had a small business, and after asking some questions invited his rescuer to his factory at Redfern the following day. For years it had been turning out things like letters from the alphabet and numerals of different sizes and colours from specially strengthened plastic. These were used in shop displays, used-car yards and kindergartens. The factory also produced a range of directional words, such as ENTER and ONE WAY, and on that first day the visitor was shown a small order of plastic exhortations – DARK- NESS, REPENT! and so forth – ready for delivery to a group of churches in Fiji. But everything about the dusty office and the factory floor where once carpet slippers had been made suggested Mr Lonsdale had lost enthusiasm; and this proved to be, for after showing the younger man around he offered him a job.

Circumstances had produced trust of a powerful kind. It was as if they had become mildly tangled up in each other's legs. The older man was always drowning. He had no family to save him. He had hollow cheeks, very noticeable.

Often they went to the races together, Rosehill, Randwick. It wasn't always necessary for them to talk.

Early on, the new arrival saw a way to broaden the firm's products. To him, aluminium represented the future. Its lightness and durability, its neutrality; a thing that can change its shape.

Here the story-teller paused.

At any other time the word *aluminium* would have been enough to send Ellen to sleep, as she had simply done with the other men who had taken their place by her bed; but she lay very still, wide awake. And she waited for him to continue. Looking straight ahead, as if she belonged to him, he casually went in under her blankets and found one of her small hands protecting a breast.

"Oh!" That was her reaction. "You're cold." It was like a block of ice with arms, this man lying beside her.

He was preparing for something; he held her hand; and, as he did, she felt her warmth overwhelm his coldness. These were Ellen's thoughts in rapid succession, and beauty began its rush back into her face.

After experimenting and researching etching processes and testing different lettering, part of the factory was converted to handle the new material, aluminium, he went on, still holding Ellen's hand, and soon orders trickled in for things like numerals for the backs of seats in sports stadiums and concert halls. But future growth pointed more towards the identification and naming of things. With the growth in higher education and leisure time there has been a corresponding emphasis on facts, almost an obsession.

We are not comfortable if a thing we have seen isn't attached to a name. An object can hardly be said to exist until it has a name, even an approximate name.

It must seem a little odd, he said, that this man in question whose instincts were towards being the naturalist – what with his studies in botany, and his years in various forests, and Kew – should become a missionary hawking the wonders of aluminium! And yet one could be of use to the other. Nameplates where words are etched into a coloured aluminium base perform well outdoors; easy to read, much cheaper than brass.

It wasn't difficult to convince the Botanic Gardens in Sydney, where the white-on-brown botanical names can now be seen in all weathers at the foot of just about every shrub and tree. And before long a steady demand came from other gardens in other states; zoos and national parks followed. Mr Lonsdale who used to make jokes about this alien substance in his factory was naturally pleased. He was good, a good man, she felt him nodding again.

At that moment Ellen heard what sounded like her father's steps near the door, and in haste she glanced up at the supposed stranger lying beside her; but either he hadn't heard or didn't care, for he continued talking normally – if anything, he seemed to be talking louder. With her mind partly on the door Ellen didn't quite register the words that followed.

A large order had come in from a new customer in western New South Wales, he had been saying. And when this order was completed he decided to deliver it personally. He could meet this new customer. It would mean travelling and staying overnight.

"Do you like train travel?" He squeezed Ellen's hand, to have her attention. "Very soothing. It must be what it's like being read to in bed. It must be all those sleepers."

At any rate – he returned to the story with the same loudness – we have the accidental entrepreneur seated comfortably in the carriage, which incidentally featured on the outside a fluted strip of aluminium along its full length. Safely in the luggage car was the wooden crate stacked with small panels of printed aluminium, a complete world contained in words and flat metal, packed in newspaper to avoid damage. The train began moving and he once more took out the order and ran his eye down the long list of names in the grazier's hand, one in caps, the other lower-case; more than five hundred names, in all. He knew he looked tired and untidy, but didn't care.

When he opened his eyes he found the two women opposite, both with grey hair, staring at him. In strange old crepe dresses they were like a couple of witches; he offered them an apple, cheese and biscuits, which they ate, leaving him nothing.

"The Sprunt sisters," Ellen murmured, still distracted.

As they neared their destination the older one tapped him on the knee, "On a property outside our town lives a young woman with her father, the most beautiful woman you're ever likely to see."

The other one chimed in, "The father keeps the key to her bedroom dangling around his neck like a jailer."

"Begin at the river," the older sister advised, "don't go near the house. She'll be somewhere in among the trees."

And that was the last he saw of them.

* *

On the railway platform he was too busy organising transport of the heavy crate to think about anyone's daughter, even if she was beautiful. This delivery was going to take longer than he thought. He began to wonder if it had been such a good idea after all. At the front gate of the property he met a Chinese man hurrying out, who nodded politely. But waiting at the door the man of the house welcomed him. "Together we unpacked the names on the verandah."

Even then Ellen could think only of her father and Mr Cave in the passage, and the true hopelessness of her situation, even though he was on the bed beside her, holding her hand.

"I remember you came out with the tea, looking *very* unhappy. I'd even say you looked bad-tempered, which may have been why your father didn't introduce me. Besides, we were busy with all those stacks of metal plates, ticking off the tree names I'd printed."

Now Ellen stared at him, then at the door, and back again. As she sat up one of her shoulders became exposed, a part of herself known to be smooth.

So much for all his worldly travels: never then had he seen anyone as beautiful.

He was touching her cheek. "Do you know what I just said? What it means?"

Very matter-of-fact, not bothering to whisper, he took her by the waist. "There was not a single mistake."

Still Ellen didn't know what to say. Above all, she was conscious again of their ease together. She felt the strength behind his hand; he was determined.

He had to say it again, "All the trees named, every single one of them. A difficult job, but not impossible. And now here I am. I could throw you over one shoulder and march off into the trees, or something like that."

He said other things. It was a matter of deciding and leaving together, *E. confluens*.

Ellen paused. That was her father moving about on the other side of the door. Before, she had heard him talking to Mr Cave.

On the verandah he considered the outline of shapes before him, semicircular in a feathery sense, darker against the sky. These of course were some of the many different species of trees, described by their different names. Did things continue to grow, even at night? A forest is language; accumulated years.

Towards town very faintly a dog barked.

Behind him he could hear Ellen humming, as she dressed. He was a man interested at a point where he felt his story beginning all over again.